MW01331580

# The I Am Assignment

Sheldon R. Smith

Cover photo by SRB Publications



SRB Publications
P.O. Box 173
Kirbyville, TX 75956
www.srbpublications.webs.com

*To the Father from his son, thanking You for Who You are in my life. Without You I am nothing, and to You be the Glory.*

*For Bobbi Miller, Kristi Clark, Laura Adams and the sociological perspectives in class.*

*G.J. Brown, thanks a million with much gratitude and gratefulness.*

I started this work back in my sophomore year of college in 2010-2011. This book came about as a result of the studies of sociology, and I started it only to lose interest in it. So, fast forward three years later, I saw how I could make it interesting as the perspectives of the sociological studies grew, and with that I was able to complete it. It is my utmost desire that you would share in seeing how a teacher was willing to vouch for his students in the midst of adversity in order to ensure them that they would go out into the world and shine as the stars that they are.

*Heroic acts aren't defined simply by the many feats*
*Nor inscribed in one's many bravados*
*Essence and truth of action are defined and depicted*
*In the heart and character of man's virtue*
*That in its moment of time is the actuality of hero*

# 1

*JUST A FEW more minutes,* I thought to myself as I peered at my alarm clock. It was 5:28 in the morning, another day. I looked over at my wife, Tracy, as she lay silently beside me. Sleeping peacefully, her serene face was so beautiful.

Knowing I had to get up sooner rather than later, I sighed and went into the bathroom to take my morning shower. We had a his-and-her bath – that was a relief. I didn't have to worry about Tracy and all of her beauty paraphernalia crowding my personal space. As I brushed my teeth, I was trying to decide on what to have for breakfast. Whatever it was it would have to be quick. Tracy rarely cooked in the mornings since we had such busy schedules. I needed to be at the school by seven-thirty and Tracy by nine. I finished brushing my teeth and jumped into the shower.

"How long you been up?"

It was Tracy. She startled me by opening the shower curtain.

"Uh, maybe fifteen minutes," I said.

She looked sexy in her lavender silk gown. I watched her walk over to the mirror to do her normal morning facial inspection. She did the same thing just about every morning.

Tracy had long, silky black hair. She always made sure it looked classy so she could keep up with the other teachers at school. She favored one of those sexy swimsuit models with her long eyelashes and narrow face. Her cheekbones were high and coalesced perfectly with her amber skin. She was my baby and I loved her to eternity and back.

When I was finished in the bathroom, I made my way to the kitchen and poured myself a bowl of Frosted Flakes for breakfast. I looked in the refrigerator for some orange juice. There was about a fourth of it left in the carton. I sat down at the breakfast table, which was next to our deck. As I ate my cereal, I began to think about the encounters of the day that I would face.

I was a sociology teacher at Lawrence Higgins High School in Madison, Mississippi. I taught on social structure, changes in social arrangements and institution, and the influences of human behavior in our society. Some would project my studies along the lines of college curriculum, but my students still seemed to grasp so much from our intense discussions of the real world. We enjoyed doing in-depth studies about why our society behaves the way it does.

I would often come home and unravel my day to Tracy. She always listened, but she had a busy business day to unwind from herself. She was a middle school counselor at Hawkin Heights Middle School over in Vicksburg. She majored in child psychology at

Jackson State University, the same school that I had graduated from. I met Tracy during my junior year at Jackson State. While I was interested in the social changes of the world, she was interested in the study of child and teenage behavior. I guess you could say that we were meant for each other seeing how we were both intrigued by the science behind human action?

"Honey, you really should get going," Tracy said, finally coming out of the bedroom.

She wore a soft purple pant suit and heels to mark her style, the image of an elegant teacher.

"You're dressed awfully early," I commented.

She started a pot of coffee. The remainders of it would probably go to waste before the day was done.

"Yeah, I think I'm going to try to get to the school kind of early," Tracy said. "Shouldn't you have left a while ago?"

She was implying that I was going to be late.

"Yeah, I should have," I said, "but the kids will need at least ten minutes to get settled."

Some days I would get to the school at seven-fifteen to "adjust" myself for the day. On days like today I would get there by seven-thirty. I lived in Jackson, Mississippi. Madison was twenty miles north of here. My first period class was a good group of kids, so I didn't have to worry about them too much.

I gave Tracy a kiss on the cheek as I walked out the side door and into the garage. It was slightly cool this morning and the sky was crystal blue. The neighborhood was quiet as the neighbors prepared for the day.

I thought about my own day as I drove through Ridgeland on my way to Madison. Feeling sluggish, I daydreamed of a life better than the one I had.

Sure, I loved my students and often looked forward to seeing them on certain days, but there were also days when I wanted more. I wanted a life where I was well known for some phenomenal event or achievement, a life where I would be well respected for touching the lives of the people I came into contact with. That was my dream and would continue to be so until I could see it become a reality.

I pulled into the parking lot of Lawrence Higgins High at five minutes to seven-thirty. I figured I would arrive later than that, but I guess my reveries sort of rushed me there faster than I thought.

Entering the building, I was greeted by Greg Maxwell. Greg taught biology and he was a calm, dignified kind of fellow. He appeared humble and modest at face value, but if you ever observed him in the middle of a serious discussion with the other teachers he could come across as cocky and brash.

"Morning, Devon," he said, going into the secretary's office. "Hope you're ready for another glorious day here at Lawrence Higgins."

Now he was being sarcastic.

"It's always a pleasure," I replied to his sarcasm.

I knew Greg felt that he had to be a better teacher than I was. I had a passion for teaching my students on the current events that make and mold us as a society.

Fourth period rolled around and I was really feeling the vibes off my students' societal recitations. We were discussing the dilemma of social identity. We talked about how we as a people viewed ourselves among others in a society where one feels that he or she must do or think a certain way to lift his or her self-image, and therefore self-esteem, in a social world. My fourth period class was the most exciting. The students were eagerly intrigued to learn more about how we could better ourselves as members of a complex society.

"I feel like if we could respect our difference, then all the other crap would work itself out," Damon blurted.

Damon was a cool kid. He stayed hip to the fashion trends and cultural changes of the world.

"What do you mean when you say 'respecting our differences'?" I asked.

Damon pondered the question.

"Well… it's like sometimes we're just too prejudice against each other beyond the black and white."

I listened avidly and allowed him to continue.

"I don't know, Mr. Waters… it's like if I act or carry myself in a certain way that might not be in agreement with the quote unquote good people of America, then I'm the one who's looked at funny."

I thought about what Damon said. As I did, I viewed the whole class and realized they all seemed to agree with him. These kids often spoke as if they wanted a chance to make a mark on the world. If that was the case, then I had to make sure I helped them do it.

"That's good, Damon," I responded. "A chance to make…"

The bell for next period interrupted me.

"All right, we'll pick up here tomorrow," I said as the students shuffled their belongings.

As they exited the room I considered Damon's words, not as a valid point made on behalf of his peers, but as a valid point made on behalf of our society.

When I left work that afternoon I decided to stop by Darby's Coffee Shop & Bar on North Lamar Street in Jackson. Darby's shop gave you a down home feeling. It was almost as if when you walked inside he'd immediately have a hot after-school meal waiting for you.

I opened the cedar door with the centered window. As I entered, the atmosphere was lulling at a dull roar. It often felt like that.

"Hey, my man," Darby jeered as I walked to the counter.

Darby was in his mid-sixties. You could tell by the gray in his hair, which resembled a perfectly matted spider web.

"How's it goin'?" Darby asked.

"Well… it's going." I rested the back of my elbows against the granite counter as I eased down onto a stool. "Say, let me get a shot of your coffee there."

Darby poured me a fresh cup of his original roast. I could tell the freshness of it by the steam rising from it as he poured. He placed the cup beside my left elbow. I took a sip.

"Hmm," I mumbled, savoring the roast as it just barely singed the tip of my tongue.

I looked out over the shop and observed the country setting. The cedar walls were glossed and the cherry wood tables and chairs sat parallel to each other. Each square table had a white and red checkered cloth draped over it. I noticed how the ceiling fans moved harmoniously at the same speed.

"What's on your mind, youngblood?" Darby asked.

"I-I don't know... you ever felt like being the hero?"

Darby looked perplexed. "Hero?"

"You know, like being the one that everyone respects because you achieved something great?"

Darby gave me that play-along look. It was as if he didn't have a clue what I was trying to say, but didn't want to offend me with his ignorance. I turned on my stool to face him. He could tell that I was about to explain myself.

"Today at school we did a study on social identity. One of my students made a comment about how he feels that he receives social prejudices from his surroundings because society as a whole doesn't respect individualism."

"Individualism?" Darby said, trying to filter through my social lingo and make sense of the matter. "Look, I don't know much about all this social identity and prejudices, but if you feel like that then maybe you ought to do something about it. Protest or form a, uh, social club or somethin'.

Darby's suggestions ignited a fire inside me.

"That does sound good," I pondered. I felt like a young lad receiving age old advice from a seasoned veteran. "I'll have to see what I can do with that," I added.

Darby grabbed his towel and continued to run it across whatever residue was on the counter. "Good. When you do come back, you can tell me all about it."

I arose from the bar with newfound confidence.

I wanted to find a way to make my students' right to individuality be voiced and heard.

I left Darby's place and got inside my Honda Civic. I couldn't wait to get home and share the good news with Tracy.

# 2

AS I PULLED into my driveway, I noticed that it was time to water the flowers again. I had a large bed of tulips planted in front of my dining room window. They were neatly planted in front of two shrubs that sat on either side of the window frame.

I walked up my brick steps to find a note taped to the front door.

*Hey Dev,*

*I'll be a little late tonight. Had a few errands to run for the house. Try to be home as soon as I can.*

*-Tracy*

She must have stopped by the house earlier, I thought to myself. I went inside and headed to the kitchen to find a snack.

I opened the stainless steel refrigerator door.

There was leftover pork chops smothered in gravy from the night before and similarly smothered potatoes with baby carrots in a container next to it. Also, there was some blackberry pie in a pan on the shelf below the pork chops. I decided to try my luck with the pie.

Tracy didn't get home until 6:30 that evening. We had takeout for dinner and retired to the bedroom to wind down. It was five after nine when we began to settle in. We didn't chatter much at dinner; usually the climax of our conversation came just before turning out the lights. We'd often discuss work and our opinions about certain work-related issues. Tracy couldn't delve too much in her discussion of the students because her work was confidential.

I flipped through the channels on the television in our room as I waited for Tracy to get out of the shower. An episode of *Forensic Files* was playing. I was often fascinated by the murder-mystery angle of this show. After what seemed like hours, Tracy finally came out of the bathroom.

"Forensic Files, huh," she said, drying her long wet hair with a bath towel. "I don't see why you like this show so much."

"Well, it's amusing," I replied. "You learn how forensic scientists solve cases long after they've been committed."

I turned off the television as Tracy crawled into bed. This was the part of the night where we discussed events from the day.

"So, how was school?" Tracy asked.

"Ah, it was good, real good. A kid's response to the lesson today has been boggling my mind."

Tracy looked alarmed. "Really… what was it?"

"Well, we were studying social identity and how the people of our society are prejudiced against one another."

"Hasn't that always been an issue?" Tracy asked.

"Yeah it has, but the response is what got me." I sat up in the bed. I knew I was about to delve into it just as I had with Darby.

"We were doing a discussion on individuality as it relates to the social prejudices of society," I started. "I asked one of the students what his thoughts were in regards to us respecting each other's differences. You know, likes and dislikes that people have towards each other, and his response was puzzling.

"He said society as a whole is prejudice towards one another beyond race. He felt that if someone thinks you should carry yourself a certain way, and you don't, then you're often viewed as abnormal and strange."

"But hasn't that always been the problem?" Tracy repeated.

"Yeah, honey, but I thought about what he said from a different angle. All the kids that we meet or see on T.V. are dealing with some sort of a complex. It could be low self-esteem, low self-image, depression, or what have you. But I believe a lot of teens, and people in general, feel this way and make bad decisions because society doesn't know the value of each person.

"We talk about the good people of America, but there's not much evidence to support our goodness toward each other. I really feel a lot of the crimes and misdemeanors of society, in regards to our young people, can be in part attributed to these impossible and duplicated images that they are supposed to uphold."

Tracy looked at me as if I was talking too fast, leaving her no room to comment or disclaimer. I'd often do that, but not on purpose. I got carried away when it came to the misconceptions of our society. That's why I loved sociology so much.

"Honey, don't you think that you're being a little too deep with these students?" Tracy said. "This isn't a college class."

"I know, but I want to come at these kids in real time from a real angle. I don't overstep my bounds and I keep the lessons congruent with the guidelines of the course curriculum. But these students don't want some watered down lesson. I have to be real with them, babe, because if I don't… then who will?"

"Well," Tracy concluded, "sounds like you've got your hands full."

"What do you mean?"

"You have a fond passion for trying to solve the riddles of a depraved society. The way I see it, this one's another one in the hat for you."

I thought she was trying to be cynical, but I wasn't sure so I decided to count it as sincerity. On that note I turned out the light and allowed our conversation to simmer down into a quiet, peaceful sleep.

*****

I would usually stop at Darby's for coffee, but I wasn't much interested in conversation this morning. Darby could talk and would talk my ear off if I went by there. My thoughts were too occupied with the discussion between Damon and myself to desire a conversation with Darby.

I started questioning myself on what I could do to better help my students. Most of them were misunderstood and often neglected. I could tell in the discussions sometimes we held in class. Either a parent, friend, or in my case, a teacher misinterpreted their expressions. For that reason, many of their actions made an open show of negligence to the world we lived in.

When I walked into the building, I headed straight for my classroom. Normally, I would stand in the hallway and chat with my fellow teachers, but today I wasn't much for it.

"Yeah, you better be glad they takin' me away," a voice yelled from around the corner from my classroom.

When I followed the sound of the disturbance, I found that two police officers had a young man in handcuffs. He was a student, apparently. I stepped against the wall to let them pass. As they did the young man looked at me as if he was waiting for me to vouch for him, but I didn't know what was going on.

I walked down the hall where students and teachers were crowded around a classroom door. It was Mr. Buckley's class. Mr. Buckley taught sophomore English. He was very dedicated to his teachings and believed that every student should give their all – one-hundred percent – in whatever they did for his class.

"What happened?" I asked Mr. Jenkins, who stood at the door marveling with the others.

"Kid got in a jab fight with Mr. Buckley," Mr.

Jenkins replied. "Obviously over some project for his class."

I was astonished. "Over a project… what happened?

"I'm not quite sure," Mr. Jenkins replied. "Maybe we'll get some clarity when this all clears out."

I tried to move closer to see what was going on. One of the teachers was helping Mr. Buckley off the floor. He had apparently been knocked down and his nose was bleeding from a punch to it.

"Excuse me, excuse me," a woman exclaimed, emerging through the crowd at the door.

It was Judy, the office secretary. She was coming to check on Mr. Buckley. I thought it was kind of late for that, seeing how the police had already come and picked up the student. Maybe she had been too frightened to show her face sooner, for fear of getting harmed in the line of duty.

When the commotion calmed, I met up with the other teachers in the teacher's lounge. I told my first period class that I had to step out for a moment and would return shortly. I didn't worry about my students acting insane while I was gone; most of them were still trying to wake up.

When I walked into the lounge there were three other teachers in there mumbling over the previous incident while sipping coffee. There was Mrs. Ettore, the Spanish teacher; Mrs. Heist the World Geography teacher; and Greg Maxwell, the Biology teacher. Greg always loved to get in the mix of conversations with other teachers – that's how he kept up to par with the current events.

I walked over to Greg. "Hey, Greg, you mind if

I talk to you for a minute?"

He pulled away from the conversation at hand and I knew he hated it. Still, he walked willingly into the corner of the room with me.

"What was that altercation with Mr. Buckley all about?" I asked.

"Some kid did a report on some record producer," Greg replied between sips of coffee. "Well, obviously he had a problem with Mr. Buckley and he decided to show it."

"There had to have been some reason," I interjected. "I mean, he couldn't have just punched Mr. Buckley for no reason."

Greg smirked subtly. "Well, apparently Mr. Buckley has rules and procedures to follow in his class and the kid must not have wanted to adhere to those rules, deciding instead to take matters into his own hands."

I ended my conversation with Greg. He seemed to insinuate a hidden agenda and I didn't want to stand around and fancy that idea. So I left out of the lounge and returned to check on my students.

By the end of the day, I was relieved. My mind had been rolling over the events of the morning's dilemma. Something just didn't add up. None of the teachers wanted to tell me what really happened, but I'd find out the truth in due time.

I decided to stop by Darby's before going home. I needed someone to alleviate my distress to. Darby was always a maestro when it came to that.

The shop was busier than usual when I walked in. Darby was chattering with one of his customers, but walked toward the bar when he saw me coming.

"Hey Devon," he said cheerfully. "Whas happenin'? How's my favorite customer?"

"Puzzled," I replied dryly.

"Uh-oh, what is it this time?"

I beckoned for a cup of coffee before I let loose the news. I took a sip as I gathered my thoughts on where to start.

"A kid got arrested today at school," I said.

"For what?" Darby exclaimed.

"Uh…they said he got into a squabble with one of the teachers. I don't know if it really was a squabble, but he knocked the teacher down."

Darby placed his hand on his chest, as if he were in shock.

"I tried to find out the whole story but none of the other teachers would freely share the details."

"A kid knocking down a teacher," Darby said. "Well, you got some out there that'll do those kinds of things."

"Yeah, but from what I gathered they told me the kid did a report on a record producer. I guess it was an English project or something. They said that Mr. Buckley, the English teacher, asked the kid to step out in the hall. He must have said something that provoked the kid to hit him."

I took another sip of my coffee as I tried to settle my mind down.

"Now, surely someone knows what happened," Darby said. "A kid's not gonna hit a teacher for nothin'."

"Yeah they know," I added. "And, before long, I'ma know too."

I took my last sip of coffee and sat my cup down firmly. "Gotta go, Darby. I need to be heading on home."

"Well, when you find somethin' out let me know," Darby replied.

He didn't have to worry about that. I'd be sure to let him and others know what really happened. I left Darby's shop with a strong desire to get some answers, and you'd better believe that I'd get them too.

# 3

AS I RODE down West Pearl Street there were a couple of kids in the front yard playing basketball. Young black and white youth, maybe twelve or thirteen, playing one on one and giving it all they had. I thought to myself on the potential that those young men possessed and how one day they would dream of playing professional basketball.

Mr. Harrison, who lived just down the road from those young men, was out watering the lawn. He'd often pass down my street to take his grandkids to Hamington Park off West Pearl and Central. He was a kind man who would often have encouraging words to say.

I took a moment to reflect on all the people who lived around me and I thought about how we had an awesome community of talented people. The only problem that dominated this community was self – looking out for me and mine and no one else. I yearned so badly to break that illiberal mindset. I was still just unsatisfied with it all. The young man's arrest at school, the struggle for social independence, and a unique individuality… these all seemed so impossible to obtain. These reflections troubled me and nagged at my consciousness.

Tracy was home. I figured I'd better get myself together before going inside. I didn't want to wallow in pity in front of her. I'd save all of my cares and concerns for our before-bed discussion.

"Hi, honey," I said, coming in through the side door. I kissed her on the cheek as I sat my things down.

The perfume Tracy wore gave off a sweet smell. I couldn't tell the fragrance. Tracy kept a varied collection of perfumes.

"Hard day?" Tracy replied.

"Meh, sort of."

I headed to the refrigerator to grab something to drink. There was no need in snacking because Tracy was preparing dinner. She had candied yams, turnip greens, and chicken in rice cooking on the stove. There was also the smell of roast beef in the oven. I had to give it to her – Tracy could cook.

"Wow, you must be in a cooking mood?" I said.

"Well, somewhat," Tracy replied. "I mean it ain't every day that we get to do this."

And we didn't due to our work schedules. However, Tracy said that cooking was a way to relieve her mind from the cares of a busy work day. It must have been one of those days, I thought.

She walked toward me as I embraced her deeply and gave her a kiss.

"Babe, you didn't have to do this," I said. "Aren't you tired from work?"

"Yeah, a little. But we can rest later."

I started thinking about how much I loved this woman. She was a gift from God, in my opinion.

"So, this hard day you had… you feel like talking about it?" Tracy asked.

I didn't at the time, but I could tell that she was concerned.

"A kid got arrested at school today."

"Arrested? For what?"

"I don't know, a lot of the teachers just tip-toed around the issue." I could sense the grievance reoccurring. "But I'll find out the story tomorrow."

"A kid got arrested," Tracy repeated, pondering the issue.

"Yeah, they said he hit a teacher," I interjected. "They said it had something to do with the student doing a report on a record producer, and I don't know if the teacher and he got into an argument, but he hit the teacher."

"That's crazy," Tracy commented, walking back to the stove.

I walked into the great room to watch T.V. until the food was ready. I propped my feet on the coffee table and turned the station to CNN. More bad news in society, and the way I was feeling I didn't need any more bad news.

"Dinner's ready, Dev," Tracy called from the kitchen.

I went into the kitchen and started putting my plate together. I wasn't one of those husbands who felt that it was his wife's responsibility to have his plate already prepared for him. I figured if Tracy had done the work of fixing the food, then it wouldn't hurt me to fix my own plate.

Whenever we had company over we would eat in the dining room, but if it was just us we ate at the breakfast table.

"Sure smells good," I said, picking up the fork.

And it looked excellent as well. The golden orange yams were glazed in a cinnamon syrup and sitting next to the turnip greens. The roast beef was cut and layered neatly, centering both of the sides. This would be a tasty meal that would hopefully help me forget my worries.

Tracy finally sat down and we ate our meal, conversing every now and then. We would save the bulk of our discussions for when we went to bed.

"You mean to tell me that's what that whole issue was about?" I said, sitting on the side of the bed.

I was talking to Felix on the phone. Felix was a janitor at Lawrence Higgins High. We became good friends maybe a year or so ago when I would stay after school and do paperwork. He would come into my classroom and empty the trash can, often shooting a word or two at me about some incident he had seen at the school.

Felix was now telling me about what happened between Mr. Buckley and the young man.

"You have got to be kidding me," I said, looking over my shoulder to see Tracy getting into the bed.

I could tell by the way she was rubbing my left shoulder that it was time for me to call it a day.

"Look, Felix, I gotta go," I said. "But, I'll get on that in the morning. Okay… I'll see you tomorrow…

all right man… bye."

I hung up the phone and stretched out.

"What was that all about?" Tracy asked, propping her head against the pillow.

"That Buckley incident," I replied.

Tracy looked at me waiting for the details.

"Felix told me that the whole ordeal was behind this kid in Mr. Buckley's English class doing a report over a celebrity record producer who held a charity fund last month in Canton."

Canton was a town several miles north of Jackson. I visited it once or twice but it was nothing for me to rave about.

"A charity fund?" Tracy blurted. "I don't even know of any charity fund being held by a record producer last month, let alone who the producer was."

"David James," I replied. "I haven't ever heard of him myself."

I wasn't a big music fan. I'd listen to music here and there, but I wasn't in love with it.

"Felix said that the student gave a report about how this record producer's benevolence inspired him. I guess Mr. Buckley's views were conflicting, and they got into it in the classroom. Mr. Buckley called the student out in the hall, said something apparently, and the kid retaliated. Now what he said… that's the question."

"But why would Buckley even go there?" Tracy said. "I mean, here you have a kid being inspired by a celebrity who's doing something positive. That's a great mark considering the stigma of celebrities in society today."

I pondered Tracy's remarks. Today's celeb society was rather shaky, considering all the slanders and scandals celebrities face.

"Yeah, well I'll further explore this issue tomorrow and in the days to come," I said.

I rolled over and so did Tracy to turn out the lights and quietly contemplate the issue within.

# 4

*I walked down the hall of Mr. Buckley's English class. I saw the kid being carried away by two police officers.*

*"You've already arrested him once," I said.*

*"Mind your business," one of the officer's replied.*

*They passed by me as I backed against the wall to let them pass. I kept walking to Mr. Buckley's classroom. As I walked, there were two lines of students moving parallel to each other in my direction.*

*They were holding large posters with different sayings on them.* ***WHY DON'T I HAVE A VOICE, CELEBRITY STATUS IS DEAD, CELEBRITY CORRUPTION STOLE MY IDENTITY***

*The students marched and chanted slanderous remarks in regard to how they felt in the matter of the student verses Mr. Buckley. These kids felt like they didn't have a voice in this world. It amazed me how the images and fads of society had caused so many individuals to stray away from their true identity, hiding behind glamour and some sort of a false hope appearing real.*

*I gaped in awe as I stood against the wall, viewing this whole phenomenon. As I continued on to Mr. Buckley's classroom, it seemed as if I couldn't get there fast enough.*

*The door to his room was closed and I turned the knob to thrust it open. When I did, Mr. Buckley was sitting at his desk grading papers, totally unconcerned with the protest outside. When I walked to his desk to say something to him, he looked up at me with rancorous eyes.*

*"What are you gonna do?" he said.*

I jolted straight up with sweat dampening my face. It was 4:19 on the alarm clock. Tracy laid there motionless and undisturbed. I sat up on the side of the bed, trying to make sense of the dream I just had. Was this a sign? Could this be my chance to make a difference? Maybe it was just the social tensions and injustices being knitted together in my subconscious.

I laid back down to go to sleep, but for some reason the memories of my dream wouldn't allow me to keep my eyes closed. I knew I'd ponder it for the rest of the night – what was left of the night, anyway.

I sat at the breakfast table, staring out at the deck as Tracy cooked breakfast. My aloof expression gave perfect definition to the way I felt.

"Honey, you care for eggs?" Tracy asked, startling me out of my in-depth thoughts and sentiments.

"Yeah, that's fine, babe."

Tracy rarely cooked in the mornings unless she had the extra time to spare, or it was the weekend. She placed my plate on the table in front of me as I continued to gaze out the window.

"Dev, you okay?"

"Yeah… I'll be fine," I lied, trying to shake it off.

"You look like you had a rough night," Tracy said.

"Ah, just a little tired," I replied. "But I'll be okay."

We had a silent breakfast, only slipping in a word or two every now and then. Afterwards, I gathered my things and headed to the school.

I arrived at the campus a little earlier than usual. Some of the students were making small talk in the parking lot while others were headed inside to get ready for first period. I felt sluggish as I stepped out of the car and started toward the building.

That dream last night had me perplexed. I had to let it pass, otherwise it would affect my teaching. As I walked along the parking lot, I spotted Dr. Charles Spartz a few feet away from me.

Dr. Spartz was a professor at Marshall Williams University in Hattiesburg, Mississippi. He graduated with a master's degree in anthropology and had been a teacher of anthropology for more than thirty years.

"Good morning, Dr. Spartz," I said. "What brings you here?"

He looked at me through small, circle-framed glasses as his face beamed with wisdom and intellect. Dr. Spartz was an older man with aged gray hair and a trimmed beard to match.

"There's the Wise Students Wise Decisions program going on this morning," he said. "The school asked me to come and be one of the speakers."

The Wise Students Wise Decisions program

was held every year here at Lawrence Higgins High. It was a program that helped motivate and encourage students to think wisely about the future and to help direct them in career thinking decisions after high school.

"So they asked you to speak, huh?" I said.

"That's right," Dr. Spartz replied. "You look a little peaky… is everything all right?"

"Uh, just got a few things on my mind that's all," I replied.

"Well, if you need someone to express yourself to, feel free to vent and share."

He continued on and went into the building. Maybe I needed to convey my troubles to Dr. Spartz. I'm pretty sure his vastness of discretion and foresight would be medicine to my mind.

As I entered the building, the halls were quiet. I walked into my room and placed my things on the desk. The students were silent and looked as if they had just lost their best friend.

"Good morning, students. Today we will begin our lesson with the discussion of social individualism."

They all gave me that "who cares" face. I disregarded it and continued.

"When we talk about individualism, we have to consider the cultural aspect of society. We know and understand that when we talk about culture, we are talking about the beliefs and values that shape and form a group of people's way of life.

"As a society, we have been dissected into so many different groups. Everything from color to culture to attitudes; there has been a great deal of division. Thus, this brings about the subject of individualism."

"Got that right," someone said.

I turned to see who it was. It was Anthony Jones, one of my quieter students.

"I see you agree strongly, Mr. Jones," I said. "Care to tell us why?"

He stared vaguely. "No, not in particular."

"Well, there must be some reason… from the sound of it you seem a little unsettled."

"Nah, I ain't unsettled," Anthony replied. "Just these cops harassin' a couple of students that's all."

I could feel the tension arising. This was a case of one student conveying his animosity for a fellow student.

"A prejudice problem, huh?" I said. "Well… Mr. Jones prejudices have always been a problem, even beyond just color connotations and all that. And this will probably resonate to the end of time, but social individualism – that's a little different."

"Social individualism? Tell me how a person can be individual, be his own person, and get hounded by some cops? You call that individualism? Man, please."

Anthony's anger had kindled. He was now making references to yesterday's incident. The sum of my dream.

"Tell me, Mr. Waters," Anthony continued. "How a kid can do a report over a celebrity doin' a charity event and some so-called teacher has a problem with that? I don't know, Mr. Waters, that don't sound like individualism to me."

I was speechless. I too felt that the actions taken in regard to yesterday's incident were alarming. I had to be careful in my proceeding speech for the fear of this argument escalating. I had to let it quiet down even though I didn't want to.

"Uh, Anthony, look... I'm not too happy about what occurred yesterday either," I reasoned. "But, you can't let one incident defect who you are as a person."

I wasn't sure I was making sense to him. "We could rant and rave about yesterday's events for the rest of the semester, but how far would that get us?"

"So what, are we supposed to just pretend like nothin' happened?" Anthony exclaimed.

"No, Anthony, because at the right time the conclusion of this whole dilemma will be resolved." I walked closer to his desk, feeling the motivation dispersing from me. "All you can do, I can do, or anyone else can do now right now, in light of what's happened, is to see how you can use this incident as an opportunity for personal growth and freedom of individualistic expression.

"In essence, taking something seemingly bad and using it for good."

Anthony gave me an expression of blind fury. "That's good, Mr. Waters, but after sayin' all of that... what are you gonna do about it?"

I froze. It felt as if a knife had pierced me in the chest. The words from my dream had now came back to haunt me, except this time it was through Anthony. I was astounded and the only thing I could hear, echoing from within, was those words.

*"What are you gonna do about it?"*

The bell rang and the students gathered their belongings, dismissing themselves for their next period class.

During my lunch break, I sat on the bench outside while drinking a cup of coffee. I wasn't too hungry and my mind was still occupied. I was deeply contemplating what I could and really wanted to do about the matter.

"Everything all right?" someone said, tapping me on the shoulder.

It was Dr. Spartz.

"Hey, Dr. Spartz, how are you?"

"Oh, I'm doing pretty good I guess," he replied. He stared at me, examining my countenance. "You don't look okay, though."

I sighed. "Well… you got a minute, Doc?"

"Sure," Dr. Spartz said, sitting beside me. I felt very gracious sitting in the presence of one of the most knowledgeable men I knew.

"What's on your mind?" he asked kindly.

I exhaled softly.

"Dr. Spartz, it's this dream I had," I said, troubled. "I'm pretty sure you've heard about the incident with the young man yesterday?"

Dr. Spartz nodded.

"It bothered me all day yesterday, and then last night I had a dream. I dreamed the incident reoccurred."

"Reoccurred? What do you mean?" Dr. Spartz asked.

"Yesterday I was in the hallway when the police took the young man away. He looked at me as if he was implying that I was supposed to do something to help him. I couldn't do anything. I mean, what am I supposed to do when the police are taking you away for hitting a teacher? So I stood and watched as the officers carried him away."

"And where did this whole ordeal take place?" Dr. Spartz asked.

"Out in the hall," I replied. "Mr. Buckley evidently was talking to him and that's where it happened."

"Did anybody know what he said that triggered the altercation?"

"No, and that's the mystery. Anyway, last night I had a dream and the scenario replayed over again. The events unfolded in my dream just as they had in real life. The student was being carried away, except this time there were a line of other students holding picket signs and protesting in disapproval. As I stood there watching all of this and the police officers carried this kid away, he passed by me and it was different this time."

I felt the unsettled emotions arising within. "I walked on and went into Mr. Buckley's classroom. Instead of lying on the floor after being punched, he was sitting at his desk grading papers. He looked up at me, Dr. Spartz, with horrific eyes and said, 'what are you gonna do?'"

Dr. Spartz looked at me, surprised. "Whoa… that's pretty strange."

"But the problem, Doc, is that the expression in his eyes and the way he asked me what I was gonna do is what startled me. It's like… it's like he felt that I couldn't do anything about it. Almost like he had some sort of power over me."

Dr. Spartz grunted. As I talked, he stared at me as if I were transparent. At this point I did feel a little bleak.

"You know, dreams do sometimes carry with them hidden meanings, Devon," Dr. Spartz said. "Sometimes messages are relayed, or there is a sort of enigmatic depth that you may need to search out and discover."

"Whatta you mean?" I asked, perplexed.

"What I mean is that you may have a longed-for desire you wish to accomplish, or a heavy burden that you need relieved. Maybe your dreams are trying to tell you something,"

*A longed-for desire.*

I thought. Maybe this was my cue to initiate change in the world.

"You know, Dr. Spartz, just the other day I was talking to a friend of mine about doing something great to affect my surroundings and the people I encounter." I shifted my posture to face Dr. Spartz directly. "Could this be a chance to birth something new in my world?"

"Could be," Dr. Spartz replied. "Once you sit down and put the pieces of your dream together, that may very well be the desire responsible for it."

I paused, reflecting on Dr. Spartz words. Maybe my dream was providing me direction in a long-lost quest. I just had to decipher its meaning.

I looked at my watch to make sure I wasn't going over my lunch break time. "Well, Doc, I guess I'd better get back to class. Wouldn't wanna be late."

We stood up simultaneously. "Yeah, we wouldn't want that," Dr. Spartz said.

He picked up his briefcase. "Listen, when you find your answer… let me know how it goes."

He was so crafted in discretion that I couldn't help but respect and appreciate him for it.

"I sure will," I replied.

We walked together and talked as we went back inside the building.

# 5

AS I WRAPPED up the remains of the day, I managed to push through my feelings of wretchedness. Still, I was relieved when I gathered my things and exited out the door to my car.

It was fairly warm outside, but the gentle breeze felt great brushing against my face. I debated whether or not to stop by Darby's for coffee. I decided I would go on home.

I took the long route home, giving myself enough time to sort out some of the things in my head. I rode Interstate 55 in the afternoon-evening traffic. I rode through Ridgeland, a town south of Madison.

There was a community in Ridgeland that I passed that looked so infamous to me. It had a sort of poverty vibe to it. I thought about all the people who passed through that little town, wandering aimlessly from day to day. I guess my inner thirst to change lives needed to be quenched – and fast.

I turned on my street to the house, there over

on Central Street. When I pulled up in the driveway, I noticed that Tracy was home. She was standing on the front porch observing the commotion that was going on up the road.

"Hi, honey," I said, walking up the steps and greeting her with a kiss. "What's going on?"

"I don't know," Tracy replied. "I came outside to get the mail and there was a cluster of people up the street."

I frowned as we looked in that direction. "You didn't call any of the neighbors to try to find out what was going on?"

"No, Dev, I'm not nosy," Tracy replied as if I was implying that she was a gossiper.

I stared a few more minutes, and then beckoned for her to come inside.

I changed clothes and went to the computer, which was in one of our guest bedrooms. We had two guest rooms and a bonus room upstairs. Since we rarely had company, I decided to put the computer in one of the extra rooms.

I could hear Tracy rattling pans and busying herself in the kitchen. I told her we could have ordered takeout so she wouldn't have to cook. I guess she preferred to cook instead.

I opened the notebook that held all of my study material. Whenever I did a study on a particular topic or subject I would keep all of the information acquired from it in this notebook. I flipped through the papers, waiting for the computer to start up.

"What are you working on?" Tracy asked, standing in the doorjamb.

"Uh, I have a little researching I wanna do. A

couple of things on my mind."

She stared passively and gave me a nonchalant look.

"Well, I'm gonna start dinner so I'll be in the kitchen."

I nodded. She walked to the kitchen and I turned back to the computer. The argument that was being presented was this: something had been said that caused a high school student to retaliate against a teacher. Discrimination shared so many faces, from color to opinion to age and so on. It was a broad term.

In this case it was a battle between a celebrity record producer, a student's view of him, and a teacher supposedly making a statement that triggered a violent reaction. I decided to do a little study on the concept of being a celebrity.

I discovered in my research that celebrity status was also a culture. The idea of people desiring spotlighted attention, and the glam and glitz for recognition and prominence flowed through our society as a sort of viral explosion. Celebrities are recognized as iconic public figures while the notion of flaws or problems go unnoticed.

Granted, that student's report may have been on a record producer, but in that kid's eyes he was the heroic image of someone giving toward a good cause. To him, the idea of charity is what should've been celebrated, especially with the amount of flack that the music world receives today.

I engulfed myself in this study for an hour and a half until Tracy called me for dinner.

"Here I come, hon." I shut off the computer and moved to the kitchen.

"What are you studying?" Tracy asked as we sat down at the table.

"Uh, celebrities and celebrity status," I replied. "Yeah… doing some research on that." I spoke faintly, trying to shun away the idea of a discussion.

We ate and chattered randomly. My mind still reeled from the information that I had read. Maybe Dr. Spartz was right when he said my dream meant something. Maybe it was my destiny to do something about this incident at school. I could use this information about the celebrity culture and persuade the school board on how a civilization deeply rooted with traditions is now far gone.

"So, this study of celebrities, does this have something to do with that incident at school?" Tracy asked.

"Yeah, as a matter of fact it does. I figured if people knew the real art of the celebrity culture, and the positive that can be drawn from it, maybe they could see the student's paper from a positive side verses always seeing the negative."

I was determined to establish a sense of equality in this matter. Sure the student jabbing Mr. Buckley wasn't a lawful act, but I was more concerned with discovering that deeper meaning that Dr. Spartz had mentioned.

"What about you, did you run across any stories today with your kids?" I asked.

"None in particular. These kids overall are just experiencing the tyranny of those unresolved matters within. Many of them aren't being heard, some are even misunderstood, but it goes back to what you said yesterday about individuality and identity."

That was a dilemma that I was becoming more and more acquainted with. These students, and society as a whole, just need guidance and truth. I was determined to establish this direction and become one of the leading men of my time.

Later that night I laid awake thinking. I looked at Tracy, stretched out in a peaceful sleep. She always had that calm, undisturbed expression when she rested. I loved that woman deeply. She was a strong and intuitive person who took pride in everything she did.

I wanted to be that courageous husband she believed in and saw me as. That's one of the reasons I persevered in matters like I did. I liked that feeling of assurance and satisfaction that came from a job well done. I longed to be that "champion" in my society who was known for establishing a just cause in the instances of injustice or misunderstanding, especially with my students at school.

That was enough with the sentiments. It was time for sleep. As a matter of fact, it was far past time for sleep.

The next morning of class I wanted to get into some critical thinking that would jog the minds of the students. I believe that this would help in furthering the conflict between the student and teacher issue.

"Let me ask you all a question in light of our last discussion," I said to the class. "We've talked about individualism and freedom, but could we attribute many of the conflicts in this society to some sort of moral decline?"

The students stared mildly. Some pondered the

question while others gave me signs of disinterest.

"I don't know about society," someone said, sitting in the back of the room, "but I know what they did to Jackie was a moral decline."

Jackie was the student who had jabbed Mr. Buckley in the nose. I was trying to find some common ground that we could all agree upon. I knew the arrest of Jackie had stirred a lot of tension and I wanted to find out where my class was in order to better help them. I believed there to be an underlying meaning to this issue.

"Okay. For just a moment, let's consider a few things," I began. "Look beyond Jackie's paper, Mr. Buckley's stern attentiveness in grading, and even the assignment as a whole. Could we say that there is a deeper meaning? I mean, the paper that Jackie wrote was in regards to a celebrity doing a charity event, but what if we look at the contrast between these two things? What if there is a hidden undertone?"

"What are you talkin' about, Mr. Waters?" Anthony said.

"I'm talking about this: What if the dilemma was deeper than a paper or a student or a teacher? Could we somehow link this whole ordeal, or the idea of someone being in a celebrity position, to something more?"

I was beginning to bring what I had been studying into real time, allowing the class to turn their attention from a minor issue to the root problem.

"You know as I do that the role of a celebrity has had its controversies for years," I said. "What if this whole conflict was just an example of the delusion of a form of expression? What if the whole idea that we see of a celebrity has caused conflict, which is based on the negative views of being in a celebrity position?"

"So let me get this right," Anthony said. "You're sayin' that Mr. Buckley's opinionative disapproval of celebrities caused him to be harsh to a student who did a paper for someone who did something charitable?"

"Could be," I replied.

"But that's dumb," Meagan said. "I mean, the producer did host a charity event. He could've been out there pushing sex or drugs, but he was doing something to help someone else."

"That's true, Meagan," I added. "But what if, because of the negative views of celebrity statuses, the teacher graded, commented, or did whatever he did, unfairly? It all goes back to the misunderstanding of a cultural expression.

"We have been talking about social individualism, culture, and the misunderstanding of it all as a society. Could what happened with Jackie be a cultural or social individualistic circumstance? Maybe, but it's how we look at it and deal with it that counts."

I turned and walked to the board to pick up a marker. "Now, I'm going to give you an assignment. You have until next Friday to work on it, and I expect everyone to do it and turn it in."

There was a sigh of unified disgust that filled the room.

"I want you to write an essay paper," now there was a strong sound of disdain and I could hear chattering in the background. "Wait a minute, wait a minute, not just any paper. The title of the essay, and assignment, is I AM… Now, some of you may be wondering why there's a blank after the I Am. Well, in light of social identity, individualism, or celebrity, I want to know who you are in this world.

"You see, this is where we get into talking about your dreams. Celebrities shoot for stardom, so why not you? A star is simply someone who took their passion and crafted it into something extraordinary. A star could be a lawyer, an artist, a fashion designer… even a teacher. When I talk about someone being a star, I want you to look beyond clichés and stereotypes. I want you to look at the core of who you are."

Everyone stared attentively. I could feel the interest in this assignment. I was creating a stage that my class could shine from.

"Think practically," I continued, "in this assignment. If you want to be spotlighted on the red carpet, then that's fine. If you desire to be a therapist or a motivational speaker in your field, then that's fine too. Every star has mastered a craft. One day you're all going to be graduates of Lawrence Higgins High, so… what will be your role and area of stardom after you leave this place?

"What I'm looking for is some thought-out expressions that we can draw an inference from and possibly build some sort of a logical reasoning." I sat the marker on the board's ledge after I wrote and circled **THE "I AM"ASSIGNMENT**.

I turned to the students to see that they were all gazing at me with expressions of inquiry.

"After this assignment," I said. "We'll see if your minds have broadened in the terms of you and the world you live in."

The bell rang and the students began to shuffle

their belongings.

"Next Friday," I repeated. "Go ahead and get started. I want really thought-out information and not just two sentences."

As the room cleared out, I sat down and rested in my chair. Now we had a forum that could give meaning to a misunderstood, controversial issue. I couldn't wait to see the turnout of this project.

# 6

I GATHERED MY things as I wrapped up for the day. It had been a good day. I had created a proposition to build critically thought ideas for one of my classes. In all of my other period classes, we had great discussions on topics according to the chapter we were in. At the end of the long day, I felt pretty accomplished. I walked out to my car and, as I did, Greg walked along with me – I assumed that he was walking to his vehicle.

"Pretty good day, Devon?" Greg said.

"Yeah… all in a day's work." I replied.

When I got to my car, I noticed that he was still following me.

"Hey uh, Dev," Greg said. "That little… uh, incident with the kid the other day… it was kinda weird, huh?"

I assumed that he had something that he wanted to say.

"What do you mean?" I replied.

"Well, I heard a couple of your students talking about an assignment that you gave them regarding who they are," he paused, giving me a look of contempt. "If I were you, I'd be careful."

"Excuse me?" I said wryly. "Why would I need to be careful?"

"I mean you don't want to start something that could land you in a world of trouble, or something that you can't finish."

I frowned again, trying to find reason in what he was saying. He sounded as if he had some sort of a conflicting view about the assignment I gave to my class.

"Listen, I don't know what the problem you're having is," I said. "But the assignment I gave to my class was about a topic, not an issue. We're discussing issues that relate to our world and societal dispositions. If you have a problem with that, then maybe you need to do your homework on the differences between social issues and biological ones."

I wanted to let him know that, first of all, there's a difference between a minor premise and a mass conflict. Second, I wanted to make it clear that I wasn't backing down. I was going to use this assignment as a gateway to a social and cultural expression, hoping to make the school institution aware of the repression thereof.

I was teaching a group of students to look beyond the model that society had laid out for them in order to move them toward a more focused approach of who they were. The big conflict was about a student doing a report, but I wanted them to delve deeper and look within to their greater selves.

Social roles and celebrity imagery had obstructed so many people in this society. I didn't have anything against "celebrity status"; I just wanted my class to recognize that they are also important.

"Now you listen here, son," Greg said. "You just watch it now, you hear?"

"Son?" I exclaimed. "I know you don't wanna go there with me."

I opened my car door and sat inside. When I cranked up the car I noticed that Greg was staring, grimaced. It didn't matter because when he left from that parking lot he would know that I meant business.

I drove over to Vicksburg to check on Tracy at Hawkin Heights Middle School. She told me that she would be late getting off, so I decided to stop by and see if I could help her wrap up her day. Tracy could be very tedious at times with her school work. Some days she would come home exhausted after a long day.

I walked through the front door and poked my head into the front office.

"Hey, do you know if Tracy's busy now?" I asked Joni, the secretary.

"I'm not sure. I can call her up if you need her," Joni replied.

"No, that's okay. I'll just walk down to her office."

The halls were quiet as I walked to Tracy's room. The students had cleared out and were assembled outside at the bus loop. Many of the teachers had left for the day. There were several still lingering around in the halls and classrooms.

When I made it to Tracy's office she was sitting

behind her desk, going over what I assumed to be paperwork. There was a stack of papers to the right of her. I smiled and walked into the room.

"Hey, babe," I said. "Whatcha doing?"

She looked at me faintly.

"Going over these files," she replied. "What are you doing here?"

"I just came by to see if I could give you a hand on anything," I replied.

Tracy chuckled, shaking her head.

"You're gonna need more than a hand for these papers," she said, nodding her head in the direction to the stack on her desk.

"How much longer are you gonna be?" I asked.

"Probably not too much longer," Tracy replied. "How was your day?"

"It was good," I said. "I gave one of my classes an assignment behind the teacher-student issue from the other day."

"What kind of assignment?"

"Well, the students were still feeling uneasy about that incident with Jackie. One of my kids felt very opinionative, so I gave the entire class an assignment. The I Am assignment."

"I am?" Tracy said, puzzled.

"Yes, I Am. You see, I asked them to write an essay paper in regards to who they were in society. A lot of people get hung up on social and public figures, but I asked them to share what they felt like their role in society was. Whether that is being a doctor, a lawyer, actor, stylist, nurse, or what have you. The role they choose is their quote unquote celebrity role, and then they have to tell me why and how.

"I told them I wanted thorough responses and they had until the end of next week to complete the assignment. Then we'll review the responses and see if we can conclude if the incident with Jackie could be attributed to a deeper issue.

Tracy gave me a subtle look of agreement.

"That's an interesting way of routing it. I hope it works out well for you."

She placed the papers she had reviewed inside a manila folder.

"You ready to get out of here?" she asked.

"Yeah… whenever you are," I replied.

Tracy stood and walked over to a filing cabinet to place the folder inside. She left the stack of papers on the desk. As she walked to the door I pulled her to me and hugged her tight.

"Hmm, you know I love you," I said, kissing her on the cheek. "I really do."

"Don't start something now," she chuckled. "I'm just playing, I love you too, babe."

Tracy reached and turned off the light and closed the door as soon as we were outside the room. I held her hand while we walked down the hall.

Joni waved as we passed by the office window and walked out the front door. By the time we were outside, everyone was gone. The buses had made their rounds and all the teachers and students had cleared out. I walked Tracy to her car.

"You going straight home?" Tracy asked.

"Yeah, are you?"

"A parent came by the school today and told me about some issues with her daughter," Tracy said. "She asked if I'd stop by and talk to them for a few minutes."

"Really?" I replied. "Did she tell you where they stayed?"

"Yeah, she said that they lived over near the Hampton Inn & Suites off Clay Street."

"Oh, well... you think you'll be a while?" I asked.

"No, she said she didn't wanna hold me all evening, knowing that I still had things to tend to as well. So, I'll do that and then I need to go by the store."

I nodded. "I guess I'll see you when you get home."

She cranked the car, backed out, and rode away. I walked over to my car. As I did, I rehearsed the events of the day.

I started wondering if maybe the assignment I had given my class would change their views of the world. Society as a whole clashed on many issues, especially in reference to celebrity roles. I really hoped that we could come to a resolution.

# 7

WHILE TRACY COOKED dinner, I decided to do a little more research on my study of the celebrity role. I was determined to investigate this subject in order to present an open case, if need be, to the school board. I wasn't an antagonist, but I believed in fairness for everyone. Mr. Buckley's approach toward Jackie, and his reaction in return, struck me as appalling.

I was noticing how the celebrity figures were portraying themselves and their actions for a good cause whereas others hid their persona in glamour, glitz, and paparazzi performances. I saw how celebrities were portrayed and modeled as individuals who possessed enormous amounts of wealth.

The celebrity role was bigger than just those who graced the red carpet. Celebrity image was modeled everywhere. From television to sports to entertainment, anytime that massive influence could be attributed to a person that left room for notable recognition.

I decided to take a break and go downstairs to check on Tracy. As I rose from computer desk, I shook the numbness from my leg. I could smell the fumes of a delicious meal filling the air as I walked downstairs.

"Hey, babe," I said, hugging Tracy from behind.

"You get far in your research?" Tracy asked.

"Yeah somewhat," I replied. "I'm still kind of in the formulation stages. I have a few more things before I get into the heart of it."

"And what do you plan on doing with all of this research after it's gathered?"

"Well, some of it I'm gonna use in my discussion for the paper that my students have coming up. I think that if I elaborate on the subject of stardom, then it would open their minds a little more."

The phone rang as we were talking. I went and answered it.

"Hello?"

"Yes, Devon?" the voice on the other end of the phone replied.

"Yes this is he," I said.

"Mr. Waters, how are you?"

"I'm fine," I replied. "May I ask who's speaking?"

"This is Mr. Donnell, your principal. I'm sorry if I'm disturbing you this evening, but I need to speak with you about something."

I wondered if this was in regards to that incident with Mr. Buckley.

"Sure, Mr. Donnell, how can I help you?" I asked, sitting in the chair at the dinner table.

Tracy stopped stirring in the skillet on the stove and stared at me attentively to see what was going on.

"Devon, I caught wind that you were giving your first period class an assignment that could be angled around the situation from the other day with Mr. Buckley. Tell me exactly what's going on?"

I was starting to think that Greg might have reported to Mr. Donnell on that scene of ours in the parking lot. I don't know why that should strike me as surprising.

"Mr. Donnell," I said. "First of all, my assignment to the class and what happened to Mr. Buckley are two totally different things. Now I did give my students an assignment that some could deem as relating to Mr. Buckley, but the work that I gave them was based on a chapter that we're discussing as it relates to cultural expression.

"Now, to whomever you caught wind of this dilemma you can let them know that there is a distinct difference between cultural expressions and its ties, and cultural expressions used to bash in defamation of character. I assure you, Mr. Donnell, that if you need proof of what I'm doing I can take you to the book, chapter, and page to show you what I'm doing is bigger than making a mockery of the school or a complete mockery of myself."

Mr. Donnell was silent. I guess my words to him left him speechless. I wasn't trying to appear antagonistic, but I was letting him know that he needed to go back and tell whoever to get their facts straight.

"Hmm. Well, Devon… that's good," Mr. Donnell replied. "But I don't think there is a need for conflict or confrontation. All I want is for us to have an understanding, and I want you to understand that I don't want any drama behind you. Now, I understand that you're working on an assignment, but if this starts a war then I'm afraid that I'm going to have to tone it down. You understand?"

"Sure thing, Mr. Donnell," I said. "And if you wouldn't mind, could you go and tell whoever it is that you caught this from to stop making mountains of molehills, and you can quote me on that. I can see right through what they're doing and I don't appreciate it."

Mr. Donnell didn't reply. Moments later we hung up.

"What was that about?" Tracy asked.

"I bet you that Greg went and told the principal about my assignment I gave the class. I know it was him because I ran into him this afternoon in the parking lot and he was gawking."

"You told him about the assignment?"

"Not exactly. One of the students from my class was probably talking with another student about the assignment and he probably overheard them."

Tracy frowned and walked back to the stove. "I don't know, Dev, maybe you ought to rethink this whole ordeal."

"No, I'm not," I exclaimed. "This is for my students and this is about establishing an understanding in order for my students to have a voice in this society." I walked back into the great room.

I wasn't about to let Greg, Mr. Donnell, or anyone else stop me from making my point. Anthony's remarks in class the other day didn't just strike as an alarm for me to come to the realization and awareness of myself, but also for my class. The students and how they felt about themselves and the world around them was very important to me. It was a social issue.

The assignment that I had given to my class was bigger than an altercation about a celebrity figure. It was about socialization and the interpretation of social order in society in the midst of all its misconceptions, misinterpretations, and anything else that would disrupt the lives of individuals.

Tracy called for me to come and eat supper. I turned off the T.V. and went into the kitchen to the dinner table. Tracy was a master at pilaf. You could taste the blends in her seasoning.

"Babe, you really threw down with this," I said.

"Hmm, thank you," Tracy replied modestly, biting a piece of broccoli off her fork.

After dinner, I washed the dishes and walked out the front door to water over our flower bed. It was dark outside, but it needed to be done. I also noticed that the grass was growing tall in the yard. I would soon need to run the lawnmower over it.

As we prepared for bed, we reviewed the phone conversation that I had earlier. I noticed that Tracy's whole approach was for me to express myself, but to do it in moderation. I could respect that and her for that matter.

*****

"Okay, class, settle down," I said, calming down the students. This was my first period class. The class I had given the assignment to.

"All right! Yesterday we talked about – well, we were supposed to talk about moral decline. I also gave you all a research assignment, which I hope you all have somewhat started. Today we are going to talk as a class about a subject that may better help you with your papers. Remember the I AM approach is from your perspective. We're going to be talking about social grouping."

The class gave me an awkward look. Some wore puzzled expressions while others appeared to think I was insinuating some sort of sexual reference.

"When we talk about social grouping," I continued, "what exactly is a social group? And, if we define it, could we relate it to our study of the social culture?"

Everyone was silent for a moment, thinking over the question asked.

"I don't know, I guess groups that relate to society," Emily answered.

"That's true, Emily, they do relate to society. But, how can we specify a social group?"

"I guess as a group of people in society who share a common bond, or somethin'," Anthony replied.

"Correct," I replied. "It's a group sharing a bond. So, think about peer groups, friends, gangs, or… celebrities. What kind of a bond do they show? Better yet, what image do you get when you see people grouped together? They must be grouped together, because they share some sort of a bond.

"We could look at this unity and goal-making as the filling of a certain individual need. Could we say that this need relates to an individual and how he or she is making their mark in the world?

The class stared at me attentively.

"Mr. Waters, is there some sort of a point to this?" Nathan asked.

"Yes there is," I replied. "I want you to think of

this in terms of the assignment that I gave you. Is there a need to display this idea of being a public figure to social grouping? Would a celebrity fall into a social group?"

"I don't know about celebrity," Anthony said. "But I think that anyone would wanna shine like a star, or have fans and everybody around them showin' love."

I paced in front of the class, pondering Anthony's response. "I see," I said. "That's a good response, and something to be considered in light of our discussion"

"Even you, Mr. Waters," Anthony said. "You can't tell me that you wouldn't want recognition for somethin' that was worth paying attention to."

"Oh, I agree with you, Anthony," I said. "Everyone wants respect for what they do. That's why I want you to consider and ask yourself, who am I on this grand stage of life? Hollywood stars walk the red carpet, but as it relates to what I desire to do, who am I and why am I a star at what I desire?"

I walked around my desk and sat in the chair behind it. "We're having this discussion of social groups, but I want you to keep all of this in mind when you're thinking about your papers."

"So, Mr. Waters, you mean you wouldn't want attention?" Anthony interjected.

"Sure I would, Anthony," I replied. "But I'm trying to correlate the celebrity with the social group and see if we could validate the two. In this assignment, I want you to consider yourself as representing the spokesperson and voice of your part in this world. Ask yourself, how would I define myself amongst others?

"Would I say that I'm a social group? Am I an

example of social identity? These are questions you need to ask yourself as we hold these types of discussions, because in the days to come we will be aiming our discussions to back your bit of genius verses the celebrity culture. They're not necessarily to promote, or brand anything in anyway, but they're to present a reasonable analysis with a very strong support on voicing who you are."

The bell rang. The entire class time had flown by before I even knew it. I was interested in the kinds of papers this assignment would produce. As the class exited the room, Emily walked up to my desk.

"Mr. Waters, do you think that this assignment will have some significance toward the incident with Mr. Buckley and Jackie?"

"I don't know, Emily," I replied. "If the responses from the class are strong enough, then they very well could."

Emily smiled, turning to walk out the door. I smiled back as she left, thinking to myself that this assignment would give my class a chance to voice their opinions. Also, it would allow them to express a form of individualism.

I stopped by Darby's coffee shop after work and chatted with him. I was sort of in a good mood after instructing my class on the I Am assignment. When I pulled up to the shop, there weren't as many cars parked in the front as usual.

Walking inside, I noticed that there wasn't much happening. The noise was at a dull roar. There was laughter here and there as customers sat at their tables talking over coffee. Darby stood at the counter hand-wiping the granite top with a rag. I walked over and took a seat.

"Whatta ya say there, Devon?" Darby said.

"Everything's all good," I replied. "I had a good day at school, the students responded well, so I don't have any complaints."

"Really, well what else you find out about that kid and the teacher?" Darby asked.

"Darb, that's an interesting subject," I replied. "I gave my students an assignment on who they are as stars on this stage of life. I guess a couple of my students were talking it over and Greg, the biology teacher, went and ranted to the principal that my assignment would give a bad reflection on the Buckley case. He must have figured it would make matters worse.

"So I talked with Mr. Donnell, the principal, and he told me to just keep it under wraps. He allowed me to continue in my assignment, but if it caused conflict he was gonna have to stop me."

Darby shook his head and chuckled. "They just wanna give you a hard time, huh?"

I smiled. Darby poured me a cup of coffee and I spun around on the barstool to see what was going on. As I sat there, Dr. Spartz came walking through the door. He smiled at me with that sophisticated look plastered on his face.

"Devon, how are you doing, my man?" Dr. Spartz said, walking up to the bar.

"Wonderful, Dr. Spartz," I replied. "Are you doing all right this time?"

He grinned and nodded his head. "The day has gone quite well so far. However, there's not too much left of it." He chuckled to himself softly.

Dr. Spartz was a kind-hearted individual. You could tell he was a very wise and noble man. He was someone I felt that I could confide in if I needed to.

"So, what brought you all the way out here?" I asked.

"Oh, Darby and I are real good friends," Dr. Spartz replied. "Yeah, we go way back some time – years to be frankly honest."

Dr. Spartz laughed, patting Darby on the arm. Darby joined in the laughter, shaking his head while holding onto his sides.

"Doctor, did you want me to pour you up a cup?" Darby asked.

Dr. Spartz nodded and took a seat as Darby poured him a cup of coffee.

"So, Devon, how is school going?" Dr. Spartz asked.

"It's going well, Dr. Spartz. As a matter of fact, I'm real excited about an assignment that I've given to my first period class. We're studying about social groups and culture trends, and one of our trends of study is regarding the celebrity culture and it's affect on people."

Dr. Spartz smiled, glancing down at the floor. "That, my friend, is most definitely a trend that progresses over time."

I nodded in agreement.

"So… how did that dream work out with you?" Dr. Spartz asked.

"You know, Dr. Spartz," I started. "I think this assignment that I'm doing for my class is a path to becoming that hero I was telling you about the other day. That whole incident with Mr. Buckley, to me, was bigger than a teacher and student issue. I believe, and I mentioned this to my class also, that it wasn't all about the report the kid did, or squabbling with teacher. I think whatever was on that paper is what we really need to seek out.

"The celebrity world as we know it has lost its true meaning. Glamour, in the original state, was intended to give actors and actresses a platform to display talent. Now it's a stage that's built on facades and false images. The idea of being a celebrity has been tainted in so many lights. I just want my class to know that they have the same amount of celebrity potential, so to speak, to achieve whatever they desire when they do leave the halls of high school education.

"If you desire a law degree that focuses on you being a lawyer, then as that lawyer others should value, appreciate, and show gratitude to you in the same way they do towards public figures. Sometimes I think celebrity figures are like fads."

"Fads," Dr. Spartz said. "I wouldn't consider it a full flown fad, per se, but I would say that it does have implications synonymous to it."

I nodded my head in agreement with him.

"You see, Devon," Dr. Spartz continued, "that is one thing we fail to realize sometimes. You have people all the time from all over the world desiring to follow a trend, an image, or a moment based on a quote unquote popular person of society. Why do they follow these persons? Because they look at the fame and bliss that this spotlighted person possesses and the person following the celebrity tries to imitate and elevate their lives to this end. To a degree, whether the person says it or not, the person that follows the public figure may in some ways feel that the celebrity is a greater person than them.

"Why would someone feel like that? A person feels like that because it's easier to follow the path of least resistance instead of blazing your own trail of stardom and work from there. Fads make a grand appearance, influence for a little while, and then disappear. A trend, however, changes form over a period of time, but yet it still follows a course. Its form can transform from generation to generation, and that is what has happened to the celebrity community."

I listened as Dr. Spartz spoke and what he said started to make sense. Darby stared at the both of us, intensely trying to keep up with the depth of our lingo. Dr. Spartz was a deep speaker; I didn't consider myself to be all that deep.

"Well, gentlemen, I think it's time for me to be moving along," I said. "Tracy might get to wondering where I am." I placed my tab on the bar counter for Darby as I stood up.

"Yeah, we wouldn't want you in any kind of trouble," Dr. Spartz said.

"Yes sir, I don't want you in a stooper on account of me," Darby added.

"Doctor… we'll be in touch," I said, shaking Dr. Spartz hand. He nodded and I said my goodbyes as I walked out the door.

When I stepped outside, I noticed the sun was shifting further west. Evening was dawning as the temperature started to cool slightly. I sat down in the driver seat of my car and cranked up to head home.

As I rode, I reflected on the conversation Dr.

Spartz and I had. Dr. Spartz was a man of knowledge and enlightenment. I hoped that from our discussion I could find that hero inside me and establish the impact I was meant to make. Only time would tell.

# 8

AS I RODE down West Pearl Street, I considered my students again and their desire to express themselves in the midst of a controversial society. I longed deeply to do everything I could to make sure that once they had passed on from high school and into the real world they would be able to do so in a fair and honest manner.

The situation between Jackie and Mr. Buckley was causing a lot of stir. That's the dilemma that I faced with my first period class, because you had a student in another class doing a report on someone the student valued. Granted, celebrities do hold quite a bit of value, but I wanted my class to know that they held value as well.

There was an array of cars lined up over on Central Street, down the road from my house. There was also a large group of people gathered in front of a man's house. He looked to be talking to them as they stood like neighbors attending a community outreach program. Maybe it was a town meeting going on. I turned into my driveway and parked my vehicle beside Tracy's.

There were many times when I would get home and Tracy wouldn't be there. She would either be working late or at the school tending to other matters. We both had busy schedules and never really had a chance to do anything together. That was going to have to change. Tracy was my wife and I didn't want us to become workaholics who lost the zest for life.

"Hi, honey," I said, walking through the door. Tracy was sitting at the dining table with papers scattered all over it.

I greeted her with a kiss. "What are you doing?"

"Oh, just sorting through these files from the school," Tracy replied.

"What, for your kids?"

"Yeah, I needed to get this done so that I could organize them." Tracy took a group of the papers and arranged them into a stack. "I had to counsel several of the kids and I'm trying to finish these files up so I can put them into the filing cabinet at the office."

Tracy looked exhausted. Paper work could be a very tedious and tiring mental process.

"Baby, let's take a break," I said, taking her by the hand. I took a seat in the chair beside her.

"How was school?" Tracy asked.

"Good. I think that assignment for my first period class will kinda help my students put their future into perspective."

"What about your other classes?" Tracy asked. "Are they doing this also?"

"No, this is just for the first period. That's the class that seemed most disturbed about it. With my other classes, we're following the lessons according to the curriculum, so it's not like they're doing something totally different."

Tracy smiled and we leaned forward and kissed each other. I took her in my arms and gave her a big hug.

"You know I love you, don't you?" I said.

"Yeah… something like that," Tracy replied. She sniggered at her response.

I frowned slightly, but knew that she was kidding. We let each other go and I stood up. Tracy arranged the papers in front of her and stood up after me.

"Babe, let's go for a ride," I said. "You remember how we used to do back when we were in college?"

"Ride?" Tracy exclaimed. "What made you come up with that idea?"

"Well, because I miss those days where we would ride and cruise and live like there was no tomorrow. All we do is work so… I want us to do something that isn't related to school work."

Tracy smiled. It was that same smile she posed the first time I met her.

"All right," Tracy said, grabbing her keys and purse. "Let's go. You driving?"

I took the keys out of her hand. "Yeah, I'll let you ride."

I turned off the lights and locked the door. We walked out to her Hyundai. As we were riding down the street I noticed those same trail of cars still lined up on either side of the street.

People were standing in groups conversing among each other. I guessed that the "meeting" was over.

"Babe, you know who lives there?" I said.

"Yeah, that's Jerry Kendell," Tracy replied. "He's a computer processing manager for EldraTech Industries down in Brookhaven.

"How do you know him?"

"His daughter attended school in Vicksburg last year. I ran into her mother and as we got acquainted with each other she told me that she stays down the road from us."

"So, how often do you talk with her?" I asked.

"Just that one time at the school," Tracy replied. "Since her daughter left the school I haven't spoken with her."

I turned and looked out the window. I began to wonder about the prominence of this man. After seeing all of those cars and people at his home, I assumed that he had quite a bit of influence in the neighborhood. Maybe it was an influence that I was unaware of.

We rode until the sun started to set. Traffic had fallen off as the twilight of the evening sat upon us. We rode and talked like we used to. I drove up to Yazoo City. We decided to stop and have dinner at Tzi Tai Yong, a Chinese restaurant.

Tracy found it ironic that I decided to try some Chinese food. She considered me a pretty traditional guy – which I was when it came to eating – but there was always a chance for something different.

"I still can't believe that you chose this place," Tracy said.

The restaurant had an outdoor patio where Tracy, I, and several other customers sat out and dined.

"Uh, I figured you gotta do something different every now and then," I replied.

I considered this moment together with Tracy magical. This quality time together gave me a chance to reconnect with my wife on a more valuable level. It allowed time away from thinking about work and the load it carried.

A song played over the radio, and as spontaneous as I felt, Tracy and I danced to it. We danced outside, alone, enjoying each other's company just like we used to back in college.

# 9

WHEN I WALKED into my first period class the next morning, the students were chattering away. Some were sitting on their desks while others stood around.

"All right, hey, everyone settle down," I said. "I hope that some of the talk is about those papers you have due soon."

Everyone simmered and returned to their desks. I laid my book bag on my desk and walked to the board.

"Now remember, the lessons that we hold in this class," I said, picking up the marker on the ledge. "They are going to cater to this essay assignment that I have given you." I began to write on the board. "Today, we are going to talk about self concept." I wrote on the board **SELF CONCEPT AS IT RELATES TO WHO I AM.**

"Mr. Waters," someone called out from behind as I wrote on the board.

"Yes," I replied. I noticed that the call came from Ethan.

"Is there really a point to all of this?" Ethan said. "Is this Psychology or Sociology? Besides, adding to the research paper, are we really gaining any ground by doing all of these discussions?"

"Are we gaining any ground… you tell me, Ethan?" I replied. "What's your idea of gaining ground?"

Ethan looked to the floor. I knew what the purpose of this assignment was, but I wanted them to see the value in it. The class was in an uproar a few days ago about Jackie jabbing Mr. Buckley so I wanted them to move away from that occurrence and focus on a more in depth matter: Who am I?

"My idea of gaining ground," Ethan replied, "would have to be something that causes change. You know, something that gets people's attention."

"Okay, let me ask you this," I said. "What if through this assignment you could invoke change? What if what you desired to be when you graduate from the hallowed halls of high school could gain you some notoriety just like a celebrity?

"What if, Ethan, your desire to be an entrepreneur, or businessman attracted influence in the world through your efforts? You think that would grab some attention?"

"Yeah," Ethan replied. "But how? I mean, who's gonna care about me being some entrepreneur that graduated from this school?"

"What if someone did?" I exclaimed. "What if a chance opened up for someone from this school to read, or hear about your paper? What if this assignment changed a student, or a teacher's whole perspective of stardom? What would you think then?"

"I guess that would be good then," Ethan replied.

"You have to open your mind, Ethan, and that goes for the whole class. You all have to see this not only from a sociological perspective, but also from an individualistic one too. This is an opportunity for each and every one of you to express yourself. You all have to understand that you have a voice, and I'm trying to prep you for that voice when you step out into the real world.

"Stardom has been limited to the big stage, sports and entertainment, music, or television. But I believe that stardom goes deeper than that. If someone desires to be a nurse, a medical engineer, professional football player, stock broker, or any other field that you could think of, that in the individual's own right makes them a celebrity. When you take what you love and master it because you love it that is what makes you a star."

The class all took a moment to digest what I said. I could see the wheels in each mind turning.

"It's more than just an assignment," I said. "Something happened between a student and a teacher and all of you had problems with it. Now we're separating the person from the issue and focusing on the issue. As you all know, the celebrity world is a controversial platform. So why not try to make your own platform and shine from it?"

I walked around my desk and stood behind it. "Let's understand and define the 'who am I' purpose as it relates to you and the role that you play. After that, we can build on this discovery. If you all are confronted with the topic of being a celebrity or public figure, then you'll have something to say. Now this is not about starting a debate. This is about bringing clarity to a misunderstood form in culture. Do we all understand?"

The class gave me a stagnant look. I believe that everyone had a pretty clear understanding of the meaning of this assignment.

"Mr. Waters," Emily said, raising her hand. "So after we finish this assignment, can we use it to maybe bring some sort of clarity to the situation with Jackie?"

"Well, it could," I replied. "Like I said, we're not trying to start a debate or cause chaos. However, if it was brought before the right people, these papers could hold weight. Especially if it was backed by twenty students. Let's just take it in steps. Work on your essay assignments with the knowledge given to you and we'll see where it goes from there."

The bell rang, dismissing class.

"Work on your papers," I said to the class as they exited the room.

On my way home from school, I passed by Jerry Kendell's house and there were cars aligned again on both sides of the street. I decided to turn around and go back to see what this was all about. When I parked and stepped out of the car, Jerry's front yard was full of people standing and listening as he narrated from the steps of his home. I walked up with my hands in my pockets and joined the group.

Some of the people from the crowd gave me nonchalant glares and some of them stared with a hint of disdain. I listened to Jerry's speech and, from the sound of it, he seemed to be informing the people about the Buckley scenario at the school. He was saying how we as a community need to pull together and reduce the violence in public schools. I know Jackie punched Mr. Buckley in the face, but I wouldn't say that our school was one of prominent violence.

"What that young man did to Mr. Buckley was an outrage," Jerry said. "That type of behavior cannot be permitted in our school. So the kid did a paper on some big time record producer and a charity, well this music crap is what triggered it in the first place. Look at how much of a garbage society that music and this celebrity bull has caused. Calling women all kinds of derogatory names and all this paparazzi jargon; it's all just preposterous."

Jerry was very emphatic with his speech. He spoke with such force and passion, and it seemed as if there was a degree of hatred toward the celebrity world.

"So you see," he continued, "we have a clear and very pertinent example of what this celebrity trash has done to not only our teens, but also to our world. Yes, the kid got arrested – well right on! It should teach him a lesson in how not to strike a teacher, first of all. Second, it shows how this celebrity fling has its consequences. Well, maybe now he'll learn his lesson. It's brainwashing our young people's minds, folks. This celebrity jargon is brainwashing their minds."

The audience soaked up Jerry's words, marveling and savoring the whole of what he said. What he was saying about the celebrity and music world was true, but there was no reason or need to badger a person because they didn't have the knowledge that was needed in how to flow in their course of living.

"That's it for today," Jerry concluded, wrapping up his meeting. "I'll see you all next Thursday."

I became disturbed. I couldn't believe that this man was turning the people's minds like this. Jackie's reaction was very uncalled for, but no one spoke of what Mr. Buckley may have said or done to trigger it. There needed to be a balance from both sides weighing the teacher and the student's response. Jackie's response occurred for a reason, and that's what no one was talking about.

I was glad that I presented my first period class with that essay assignment because of moments like these. I wanted to walk up to Jerry and give him a piece of my mind, but I didn't. What kind of an example would I be for my students if I did that? I really hoped that when this assignment was complete that an opportunity would arise for my class to present and bring back to its rightful place the true origin of what it means to be a star.

In my eyes, this whole ordeal was bigger than a music icon, or some record producer. For Jackie to decide to do a paper on a record producer indicated that he evidently saw something in that producer that attracted his attention. I believed that the same amount of glamour and potential that celebrities in this world possessed was not just limited to the people on television. I believed that my students could be stars in whatever they desired to be – even if what they wanted to be wasn't considered as "stardom". That was the point I was going to drive home if it took the rest of my life as a teacher.

I turned and walked to my car to leave.

"That was a good meeting wasn't it?" someone

said to me as I was leaving.

I looked at the man and grinned partially. "Yeah, it's something to see."

"Are you from around here?" the man asked.

"Yes, as a matter of fact, I live right around the corner."

He walked closer to me, extending his hand. "James Watson."

I glanced at his hand briefly and thought to myself if I wanted to shake hands with someone who represented an antagonist to unclear reasoning.

"Devon Waters," I replied, shaking his hand. The modesty of my character wouldn't allow me to act unkind to his hospitality.

I mean, it wasn't his fault that he knew someone who didn't have the full truth, and was basically generating speculations and perspectives based on his own point of view.

"What kinda work do you do?" James asked.

"I'm a teacher."

"A teacher. Where do you teach?"

"I teach a Sociology course at Lawrence Higgins High School in Madison."

"Sociology," James echoed. "Well, this kinda matter we're discussing here is right up your alley."

There was some truth to that statement. I was in no way trying to tear anyone down, but I was trying to get some understanding and closure on the matter. The truth was only being told in part from one side. Everyone was talking about what Jackie did, but no one furthered the investigation into Mr. Buckley's actions.

"Well, you have a good evening, sir," I said, opening the door of my car. He said goodbye and I left.

When I turned into my driveway, I noticed that Tracy was home and someone else was parked behind her car. I pulled under the garage and walked in through the side door next to the garage.

"Hi, honey," I said, kissing Tracy on the cheek. There was a lady who looked to be about Tracy's age sitting at the dinner table.

"Babe, this is Alyssa," Tracy said. "She's a teacher from the school. We were talking about a project that we are preparing to embark on for our middle school students."

Alyssa smiled warmly. She looked soft-hearted in her character and persona.

"Yeah, we got to talking about some of the obstacles our students face on a day to day basis," Tracy said. "Alyssa saw my eagerness on the subject and wanted to get together to see if we could maybe arrange a social group project that would promote positive motivation in our students."

"That sounds good," I said. "We could really use some at our school."

"Really? What do you teach?" Alyssa asked.

"Sociology," I replied.

"Wow, that's a pretty complex subject."

"Yeah, it's just trying to get others to respect the complexity of it." I sat my bag in one of the chairs at the dinner table. I was still baffled about the discussion at Jerry's house.

"Do you have any trouble relaying the subject to your students, Mr. Waters?" Alyssa asked.

"No, it's not the students," I replied. "It's some of the faculty that problems may circulate from."

"What's the matter?"

"A student hit a teacher in the face. Yet no one's really clear on why this occurred. Everyone's ranting and raving over the issue, but no one's saying what the teacher did to cause the student's response."

"Does anyone know at least what may have caused it?" Alyssa asked.

"The whole ordeal stemmed from a paper that the class was asked to write. The student did his report over a record producer hosting a charity event in Canton last month. Whatever the teacher said ticked the student off and he jabbed him in the face."

Alyssa looked alarmed, rubbing her chin. "Wow, well…who was the teacher?"

"Wayne… Buckley," I replied. "Yeah, he teaches English at Lawrence Higgins High."

Alyssa's face showed disturbance. She looked at me as if I had said something terribly wrong.

"Alyssa, is everything okay?" Tracy asked.

"Yeah, it's just weird," Alyssa replied. "That's strange. Look, I'd better get going," Alyssa said, standing up and fumbling to gather her things. She moved offensively and in a perplexed manner.

"Okay, well call me," Tracy said. "You have my number and we'll see about arranging that project." Tracy followed Alyssa out the door.

I stared out of the window as they laughed and talked. I was a bit suspicious about Alyssa's response. Something just didn't seem right.

"What was that all about?" I asked as Tracy entered through the front door.

"What was what about?"

"Alyssa and the funny looks," I said.

"I don't know," Tracy shrugged. "Maybe she

was just concerned."

"Well, it looked a little more than concerned." I walked into the great room and sat on the couch.

"Dev, what's going on with you?" Tracy asked, walking into the room and sitting beside me.

I paused for a moment and reflected on all that had happened this evening. I thought about my talk with Dr. Spartz, the speech that Jerry Kendell gave to the fellow neighbors, and how it was all so much.

"I stopped by Jerry's house this evening," I said.

"Why, why did you go by there?" Tracy asked.

"Because I was curious. I've been seeing cars lined up on both sides of the street and I wondered what the big commotion was all about."

"Did you find anything out?" Tracy asked.

"Yeah, I did," I replied. "This man is holding a rally at his house because of what Jackie did to Mr. Buckley. So now he feels that Jackie got what he deserved."

"What do the neighbors have to do with it?"

"Support," I replied. "That's all they are." I started to get angry. I stood up and paced back and forth in front of the television.

"Dev, you gotta calm down," Tracy said.

"I can't calm down!" I exclaimed. "Everyone is going on about what Jackie did and how Jackie needs this and Jackie needs that. What about Mr. Buckley, huh? No one wants to talk about that or try to see what made this kid snap. That's what's not being talked about or investigated."

Tracy placed her elbows on her knees, rubbing the temples of her head with both hands.

"I don't know what everyone's angle is," I said,

"but I hope that my students write one heck of a paper on the subject of who they are and what makes them stars. Because at the end of the day, that's what everyone has a problem with."

Tracy stood up and walked into the kitchen. I could see that she was upset.

"Tracy, babe, I'm sorry," I said, following after her. "I didn't mean to holler at you." I walked and stood behind her, wrapping my arms around her. "It's just… it's just I hate to see how all of this is going down."

"And I hate this," Tracy snapped. She turned around and looked at me. "What about us, Devon? It seems like all we talk about is work and school." Tears now filled Tracy's eyes. "What about our lives?"

I grabbed Tracy's shoulders and pulled her to me, hugging her tight. "Babe, you're right. You're absolutely right. I… we do spend so much of our time caught up in school that we never spend time learning more about each other."

Tracy sniffed and wiped tears from her eyes. The truth of the matter was that we spent hardly any quality time together. I thought about what she said and how I was so wrapped up in this fight to prove Jackie's case that I put Tracy's feelings on the backburner.

"Trace, listen," I said. "Why don't you and I go away somewhere, just me and you?

Tracy used both hands to brush the remaining tears from her face. "Yeah, that sounds good."

As much of a teacher as I was, Tracy was my wife and I had to keep that in mind regardless of how busy the days were. I couldn't keep allowing all of this to hinder my relationship with her.

"Honey, listen to me," Tracy said, sniffing. "I know how much this assignment and your students mean to you. I just don't want you to lose yourself behind it and forget who you are."

"You're right," I replied. "It's just that I want my students to have a voice in this world, and not to get caught up in the lights, camera, and action glitz of the celebrity world. I don't want them to spend their lives boxed in a world where they lack the freedom to express who they really are. That is the purpose of this assignment; it's to show them that they are stars in a field of expertise, even if it's not in Hollywood."

I walked to Tracy and placed my arms around her. We were silent for a while, standing and hugging each other. I was glad for this moment, because it allowed me a chance to see how side-tracked I was from my wife and also it was a reality check to see if I would keep to my own identity. However, I hadn't forgotten about the matter at hand.

There was something suspicious about Alyssa, so I decided to keep her under close observation. Jerry had a great deal of influence in the community and I would need a lot of support to counteract his persuasions. But I believe with the support of my students, and the right frame of mind, we still had a chance to make leeway and offer a new voice to be heard.

# 10

WHEN I ARRIVED at the school the next day, I walked down the hall swiftly and prepared to engage into some critical thinking with my students.

"Devon," someone called out from behind me.

It was Mr. Donnell, the principal. He started in my direction with an intent look on his face.

"Devon, I wanted to talk to you about that assignment and ask how it was fairing."

I looked at the **#1 Principal** pin that was attached to the left lapel of his blue blazer, thinking to myself if there was an ulterior motive to this discussion.

"It's going good, Mr. Donnell. The students are starting to open up and really dig deep within as they consider the potential of who they are."

Mr. Donnell nodded. "That's great. Uh, Dev, I want you to be clear on something here. Now, I sincerely hope that this assignment doesn't lead to a matter of brainwashing these…"

"Brainwashing?" I exclaimed. "Mr. Donnell,

what do you mean by brainwashing? I simply posed an assignment based on a subject we're studying."

"Stardom?" Mr. Donnell said. "Celebrities? Is that what y'all are studying?"

"Social identity," I replied. "I'm trying to help my students understand their place in this world, and also how to understand role positioning as they prepare to leave high school."

Mr. Donnell frowned, pressing his lips together as if to hold his anger inside. I found no fault in what I was doing, and I was in no way violating the school's core curriculum. My approach to the subject may not have been what Mr. Donnell expected, but I hadn't broken any rules.

"All right, Devon," Mr. Donnell said "I'll let you get to your class, but the moment this thing gets blown out of proportion I'm calling it off."

I wanted so badly to give him a piece of my mind, but I had other matters more important to concern myself with.

"Yes sir," I replied, and then turned around to continue to my classroom. It was time to occupy myself with less trivial things.

"All right, class," I said when I entered, walking to the board. "We are studying the self concept. Now, I know you may be still asking how this relates to the assignment I've given you. The self concept asks the question: Who am I? Meagan, who are you?"

Meagan was one of my more prissy students. She gave the countenance of a would-be super model, but with attitude.

"I don't know," Meagan shrugged, chewing her gum as she twirled a strand of her blonde hair. "A student, I guess."

"But when you graduate this year and go out into the world to face society, who will you be presented as among other people?"

Meagan frowned, smacking repetitively on the gum in her mouth. "I don't really care what other people see me as. All I know is that I'm gonna go to school and get my license to be an RN.

"A nurse?" I said, raising an eyebrow. "So you like nursing?"

"Yeah, I guess. Why? Is something wrong with that? At least I'll be getting paid."

"No," I grinned. "No, that's good, Meagan. Now in light of our discussion of the self concept, celebrity status, and so on: How does that make you a star on the stage of life?"

The class was silent. There were expressions of critical thinking, suspense, and slight cluelessness. This was the kind of energy I wanted to create. I wanted my students to really give thought to their place in society and not get so caught up in watching public figures live in success and fame while they settled for the mundane.

"What I mean by that," I added. "Is if any celebrity, or any famous person, could take something they love and flip it until they get what they want, then why can't you get the same recognition, influence, or high profiled status for being a nurse?"

"Well, I guess I hadn't thought about that," Meagan said. "I mean, I don't see how me being a nurse could make me popular."

"Popularity is not what we're focusing on," I said. "Just think about how much influence you could have in the nursing field. You see, that's what I'm trying to get all of you as a class to understand. I don't want you to limit your success to the lifestyle of the rich and famous, so to speak. Jackie did a report on a record producer; he evidently saw something in that man that inspired him to write about him."

"Um-hum," Anthony mumbled.

"But," I continued, holding up my index finger, "why can't you all do something that people could write about?"

"Mr. Waters, do you really think that anyone cares about this whole stardom thing?" Anthony said. "We're just a group of students trying to get through this year and get the heck out of here."

"But then what?" I interjected. "Once you leave the halls of Lawrence Higgins High, what next? I know you may still be thinking, 'Mr. Waters, what does this self concept crap have to do with this paper? Or better yet, what does that have to do with that whole incident with Jackie?'"

Anthony gave me a so-what stare.

"I'll tell you what it has to do with this assignment and incident. This whole lesson, this whole discourse comes from you all showing me how displeased you were about a teacher having a student arrested. Did they need to figure out why he did what he did? Sure, but even in the midst of that whole situation, what can you do about it?

"I'm not telling you to treat it as nothing. I'm simply presenting you with an alternate outlook of the situation in a core curriculum manner. We're studying the self concept as it relates to social identity. I'm posing to you a food for thought assignment as it relates to you and your life when you leave from here."

The class listened as I spoke attentively. I wanted to direct their minds so that they could see the importance and sincerity of this assignment.

"Emily asked will this paper help out in the case of Jackie and Mr. Buckley," I said. "Who knows? But I can guarantee you that if this is presented before the board, or someone in a more authoritative position, I can show that a group of students have looked past the drama and toward a future yet to come."

I think that everyone saw where I was coming from.

"The whole idea is to present stardom in a different light," I said. "Jackie did a paper on some celebrity and the next thing you know he's getting jailed for hitting a teacher. What is your idea of stardom? What is your idea of celebrity, beyond some bright light and a big stage? Why can't stardom or celebrity status be considered from the perspective of the personnel consultant? The psychologist? The sports manager, or the cosmetologist? What about even the nurse?"

I looked at Meagan as she connected to what I was saying. "Think about what it is that you aspire to be and how it can be, in your own right, linked to stardom."

The bell rang.

"Think about that for your papers," I ended. The students shuffled their books and exited the room.

I stopped by Beckon Auto Center off of Highway 51 in Madison after school to get my car serviced. It was past the time to get that done. I was always on the go, so it was hard to find the time to do so. Soon it would be time to get my tires changed also.

When I walked into the place, there was the smell of rubber in the air. There were four blue plastic chairs on either side of the glass door. I walked up to the wood-grained counter to speak with the gentleman about getting serviced.

"Hello, sir," the man behind the counter said. "What can I do for you today?"

I looked at the white name tag on the left chest corner of his shirt. It read FRANK.

"I'm doing good, Frank. I'm here to get a service job done to my car," I replied. "I need an oil change. It's actually past time for that," I chuckled.

He took my information and the keys to my car. I walked over and took a seat, picking up one of the magazines to look through it. I called Tracy while I was sitting there to let her know where I was in case she made it home before I did.

"Yeah, I think that size would be a better fit," someone said, entering from the side door of to the service center.

I couldn't believe who it was, at least not in this place and at this time.

"How are you?" Jerry Kendell said, taking a seat on the other side of the room.

"Good," I replied.

He picked up a magazine, as well. I assumed that he was getting his tires changed. Why was he here in Madison when he worked in Brookhaven?

"Yeah, that's gonna look good on your truck, Jerry," Frank said.

I used my peripherals to stare through the side door glass. Jerry drove a big Ford King Ranch truck. It was a bright strawberry red and something that made him look the part of a big shot.

"Driving back and forth from Brookhaven to Jackson has caught up with my truck," Jerry laughed. "A lot of times I drive that route seven days a week."

I was feeling kind of chatty, seeing that this was the same man stirring a riot in our town.

"Excuse me, sir," I started. "Are you from Jackson?"

Jerry gave me a peculiar glare. "Yes, I am. Why?"

"Oh, no particular reason," I lied. "It's just that I'm from Jackson, too."

"Really? Well I work down in Brookhaven, but I get a lot of service work done here in Madison. Yeah, Frank is a good friend of mine," Jerry smirked. "He takes real good care of me."

Frank grinned. They looked as if they were close pals. Jerry seemed like an all right person, but it was his antagonistic approach that I disliked.

"I hear you, well I'm a school teacher," I chimed.

"Really? What school?" Jerry asked.

"Lawrence Higgins High. I teach a Sociology course there."

Jerry looked as if I had said something profane. "Well now, ain't that something. I guess you heard about the kid that hit the English teacher? That's preposterous."

I raised an eyebrow, fancying Jerry's use of big words. "Now, it did cause a stir, but my biggest question is what did Mr. Buckley say that made the kid hit him?"

"Doesn't matter," Jerry replied fervently. "All I

know is the kid did some paper over some celebrity. He's supposed to be some big name." Jerry turned his seat toward my direction, shaking his head. "Boy, I tell you, this world of celebrity trash makes some people do stupid stuff."

I could feel the anger arising in me. I closed the magazine and placed it back on the magazine rack sitting near my chair.

"I can understand the feud about celebrities," I said. "But the student was doing a report over someone who was evidently doing something for a good cause."

"Good cause or not, that boy's actions were unnecessary," Jerry interrupted. "That's a teacher."

"And I'm a teacher," I reminded Jerry. "So what? Are we excluded from doing things that provoke people? You see, I understand that the student's actions were a bit much, but what I'm having a problem with is the reason why that the student retaliated like he did. That's my concern."

Jerry stood up. "It still doesn't matter. All I know is that this kid allowed some celebrity scuff to brainwash him."

I thought on that term "brainwash". It was the same jargon that Mr. Donnell presented me with. I shook my head, standing up to get on Jerry's level.

"Celebrity scuff?" I said. "Listen here, I'm not stupid. Okay, my approach to certain things can be slightly biased, but I know that there was more to that incident than is being told. I know that you hold a little rally a couple of blocks from where I live. I sure hope, for your sake and the sake of the students, that you're weighing into account the basis of both sides… teacher and student."

"The only thing that I'm weighing into account here is honest justice. Justice that teaches these kids that there's more to life than chasing fairy tale whims that these celebrities present." Jerry put his hands on his hips and turned to face the window. "And we wonder why these kids are so messed up."

A mechanic entered through the side door. "All right, Mr. Kendell, she's ready to go."

Jerry turned and faced me. "Thank you," he replied to the mechanic while staring at me.

I walked in closer to Jerry.

"Why not offer another alternative?" I said.

Jerry frowned, so I elaborated.

"When I say alternative, I mean why not show these students that they can be stars in whatever they do when they move on from high school?"

"Alternative?" Jerry smirked, counting my speech as rhetoric, "Stars when they leave high school? Listen, I don't know what kind of high cloud you're on, but this is the real world. Your 'students'," he said, making quotations with his fingers, "need to understand that this is reality, jack. We're living in the real world. If you want to make something of your life, then you better get on the bandwagon."

"Bandwagon?" I replied. "You see, I think that is what's wrong with a lot of people in our society. Celebrity or not, bandwagons have gripped the lives of so many people."

Jerry started walking to the counter. He reached in his back pocket and pulled out his wallet to pay Frank. He put several one hundred dollar bills on the counter.

"Thanks, Frank," Jerry said and walked to the

side door. "I would love to sit here and have this extensive speech, but I have a wife to go home to."

"Until next time," I said, backing into the chair behind me and sitting down.

Jerry looked at Frank, and then at me as he walked out the door. He had a distasteful resolve, but I was in no way going to back down. The whole of the story had yet to unfold and I was going to stand my ground until the conclusion of the matter was settled.

# 11

"YEAH, HE WAS just going on and on about it," I said to Tracy. We were preparing for bed.

Tracy had cooked grilled chicken in an Italian sauce and a summer vegetable stir fry. Outside of work, Tracy could throw down in the kitchen. She had a knack for creative recipes, especially if an idea for one came from a cooking show.

I pulled the covers back and stretched out. Tracy came out of the bathroom, sprucing herself with one of her fragrances. She pulled the cover back on her side of the bed. As we both laid there, I pulled Tracy to me in a close embrace. I gave her a kiss and tightened my hug.

"Hmm, I love you so much," I said in her ear, still holding her.

"Yeah, I think you've mentioned that a time or two before," Tracy replied sarcastically.

We turned off the light and I continued to hold Tracy close to me. A street light from outside cast a dull light, shadowing the room.

"You know, babe, no matter what I do I want you to be proud of me," I said. "I know I talk a lot about those kids, but I want to do this for the both of us. I want what you do as a teacher to shine light, too."

Tracy turned and faced me. "Devon, I know you want this for your kids. There's no doubt in my mind that what you're doing is all a part of making your mark in history. I… I support you in what you do. As long as it comes from a good heart…"

I put my index finger over her lips.

"I know you do," I said. "But I also know that you're my wife, and I don't ever," I shook my head slightly. "I don't ever want to put anything above our relationship. If I have done something, if for any reason my attention has robbed the kind of affection that is due you, I'm sorry."

Tracy moved her mouth as if to say something, but I placed a finger over her lips again.

"You are my wife," I said. "You help do so much to make this house and our lives function as they're supposed to. For that, sweetheart, I am forever grateful. I love you so, so much. And as the husband of this house, I want to commit to you by doing my part so that we can both flow together in harmony"

I could see a tear trickle down Tracy's face. In the world we lived, some would consider my speech as naïve and a whimpered-over, would-be expression of a man. But I understood that Tracy and I were one. I would go to bat for my students, but Tracy was first priority above all else. I wanted her to know that, too.

Tracy kissed me.

"You try to be tough when you want to," she said, chuckling. "Honey, I know you do. I know that you want the best for these students and I can tell. I love how you're willing to shove aside the statues of status quo in order to make your mark. I believe in you. I believe in what you are doing to make a contribution into the lives of these students."

And Tracy coined that phrase correctly. My students were stars and I was going to do what I could to make them shine. We caressed each other a little longer until we fell asleep in each other's arms.

During my lunch break the next day I did some studying behind social positioning. I found in my observation that people can allow society to handwrite for them the image of who they are, what they are supposed to do, and how to carry themselves. I wasn't in total disagreement against the world we lived in; I just wanted my class to be the people they were created to be outside of the dictates of social status.

The assignment I gave to my first period class was created to expand their minds beyond the red carpet and those that graced it. I wanted them to know that no matter what they desired to do, whether it was to be a lawyer, stock broker, police officer, or a mentor for battered women, they could be stars in any of these endeavors.

As odd as it sounded, I didn't want my students to limit stardom as some place far away from them.

"Mr. Waters," someone said as I sat on the bench outside, going through papers.

I looked up and saw Nathan standing behind me. Nathan was one of my students from first period.

"Hey, Nathan," I said. "What's going on?"

"I hope I'm not disturbing you from anything,"

he said.

"No, no I was just going through some research papers," I answered, noting the puzzled look on his face. "Is everything all right, Nathan?"

"Yeah, I just had a question about the assignment you gave us," Nathan said.

A brief shot of excitement surged through my chest.

"Okay, well what can I help you with?"

"Uh, first of all, I think this is an awesome assignment," Nathan replied, "but I was kinda wondering if our efforts in this assignment would really make a difference."

I paused briefly and considered the perspective of Nathan's disposition.

"You know," I said. "There have been several people who have asked that same question, Nathan. Some are hoping that it will bring about gain and some are hoping that it'll fail. Truth be told, Nathan, this assignment was born out of a frustration that your classmates had concerning one of your fellow students. My purpose with this assignment is to get you to look beyond a situation and see where you can go in life.

"Jackie did a paper over a celebrity producer, but I want you all to find that star in you. So many people look at being a celebrity as some hype, or a faraway fairy tale that only a select few can live. But, Nathan, whatever it is that you desire to do with your life when you leave the halls of Lawrence Higgins High is your stage of stardom. This isn't some hype message I'm putting out, it's the truth."

Nathan stood there, caught up in my speech as if I had said a mouthful. I wanted the students to dream beyond where they were and go to a place above.

"Well, I hope that we make you proud, sir," Nathan said. He smiled and turned away.

"Nathan," I called out. I walked toward him and placed a hand on his shoulder. "Don't just do it for me, do it so that you can make yourself proud."

Nathan smiled again, and then turned to walk inside the building. I gathered my papers together and went back in, as well. I was starting to think that it was time to take a little trip once school dismissed. A trip that was long overdue.

# 12

I STOPPED BY the juvenile center in Hinds County, Jackson. That's where Jackie was and I thought it would be good if I had a chance to pay him a visit. When I walked inside, I spoke with the facilitator of the center and told him who I was and why I was there. I wanted to speak with Jackie and try to get the truth from his perspective. I knew there were two sides to every story, but I had yet to hear his side.

Jackie came walking out a door that led to where all the juveniles were held. He was wearing a mid-sized leather jacket, a fitted charcoal-colored shirt, and smoky gray jeans. Jackie looked as if he hadn't slept in days. His thick, curly black hair was rigid and his eyes were slightly sunken in his head. He walked to me and the security guard followed along.

"Could we have a seat over here?" I asked, pointing into the lobby area where several wooden chairs were lined side by side.

The guard hesitated but gave a nod.

"I'm only going to give you ten minutes," he said.

We walked over and sat down. I sat my book bag on the floor beside me.

"So, how you been?" I said.

Jackie stared at me.

"I've been better," he replied in a raspy tone.

"Listen, Jackie, I'm here because I want to get some answers from you. Now, I'm not here to stir up any more trouble than has been caused. I just want to hear your side and why you retaliated the way you did."

Jackie held his head down, grunting as if this were a question he had been asked multiple times over.

"Look, Mr. Waters, I don't know if my answer to that question is gonna solve anything. Okay, I did what I did because some teacher tried to put me on blast in front of the whole room."

"I mean, what did he say?" I asked.

"Doesn't matter," Jackie replied. "All I know is that he shouldn't have did what he did."

I turned my chair toward him, placing a hand on his shoulder. "Jackie, how can I help you if you don't give me anything to work with?"

Jackie jolted out of his seat.

"You can't help me!" he exclaimed. "Because, no matter what I do or say it don't mean… it don't mean a thing."

The security guard walked over to where we were. "All right, Devon, I think that's enough for now."

The guard escorted Jackie back to where he came from. Jackie would be suspended from school for a while, and would get some time in the juvenile center for his actions.

I picked up my book bag and walked out the door. As I walked to my car, I thought about the assignment I had given my students. I still didn't know why Jackie did what he did, but I had twenty students and an assignment to turn up the heat several notches.

*****

"Does anyone want to share with me some of what you've learned about yourself?" I said, waving a pen in my hand.

Jackie's events yesterday evening had me on a roll. I left that juvenile center thinking about how a kid like Jackie's whole perspective on things had been distorted. His whole life, for that matter.

This whole situation reminded me of a theory of how social roles could be accredited to a person based on some sort of false evaluation. Maybe Jackie had been written off as a misfit kid who needed nothing more than to be locked up in a delinquent facility. The dangers of society and the misconceptions they can give.

Emily raised her hand.

"Yes, Emily," I said.

Emily arranged her papers and shuffled them into a complete stack on her desk. "Well, I'm sort of getting the story together, but I think I'm on the right track."

I held out my hand, encouraging her to share what she had.

Emily's eyes shuffled back and forth as she stared at the paper. "I… I am the life coach for the broken woman," she read. "I am the one with a voice to appease the tears of heartbreak many times over. Many women in this world have been tamed and misled in so many ways. I am now, and will always be, the voice that coaches the lives of many women, leading them to the truth."

I was stunned. I couldn't believe what I was hearing coming from a student whose persona spelled "reserved" and "timid". That's the way Emily had carried herself for as long as I had known her.

"Wow, that was awesome, Emily," I said amazed, "A life coach huh?"

Emily arranged her papers again with a look of certainty. "Yeah, that's what I want," she said in a quiet tone.

I turned and walked around to the front of my desk. The rest of the room remained silent, thinking on Emily's speech.

"Now that's the kind of stuff that I'm looking for," I said. "I don't want some sound-good answer, or something that you think you can get over on me with. I listened to Emily and I could tell that she wrote from the heart. That's what I want to hear. Heart."

The class sat there in a trance. I believe that the reality of the assignment was starting to make sense.

"We have a few days left to get this done," I said. "I want you to put your all into it. Hey, this is your assignment, and not only that but your life as well. So… what are you going to do with the rest of your life?"

Anthony raised his hand. "Mr. Waters, forgive me if I'm wrong, but I'm guessin' that there's a point to all of this? I mean, it looks like we've moved from sociological studies topics into some sort of life philosophy."

Anthony was one of my more trivial students. In his world, everything was point blank. He was an either-you-are-or-you-are-not kind of person. When it came to delving into thought provoking assignments he believed in walking on the outside of the boundaries, so to speak.

"You know, Anthony, I've said this before and I'll say it again, I want you to think. Yeah, this is a Sociology course, but I also want you to think about your life outside of these four walls."

I walked from around the desk and to Anthony's desk. "Tell me," I said. "Who do you believe that you are? This is all in the connotation of social identity, so… what is your 'I am'?"

Anthony cornered me with his eyes, slouching in his seat. "You know, that's a good question," he replied sarcastically. "And right now I would love to give you an answer, but I'm just afraid that I can't give you one."

"Okay, so this assignment is due soon and you mean to tell me that you haven't thought up anything yet?"

Anthony changed positions in his seat. "Yeah, I got something," he replied, brushing on his blue Nike hoodie. "But…"

The bell rang.

"Class dismissed," Anthony concluded. The rest of the class gathered their books and backpacks.

"Reports due soon," I shouted out. "I want serious essays from the heart."

I looked at Anthony as he walked toward the door, looking back and giving me a smirk. He may have thought he was getting off easy, but time would tell.

And in that moment he would eventually lower his guard and allow reality to break through.

I rode over to Tracy's workplace in Vicksburg after school. Interstate 20 was building upon its evening traffic. Tracy told me that she would be late getting off due to an after school teachers meeting. I figured I'd give her a hand to help wrap up her day.

Jackie's whole course of events replayed through my head. I asked several students at the school what was said, but no one was really clear on it. The real nitty-gritty occurred when Mr. Buckley asked Jackie to step out in the hall for a moment. It was what was said in the hall that set this whole course of events.

I jammed on the brakes, almost hitting the car in front of me. That moment shook me out of my reverie. The combination of fast and slow with traffic was something you had to know how to flow with.

I finally traipsed on until I made it to Hawkin Heights Middle School. There were a handful of cars in the parking lot. When I located Tracy's car, I parked beside it.

When I made it to the front door, I could see classroom lights on further down the hall. The hall lights were off and the front door was locked. I meandered around the front door slowly with my hands in my pockets. Suddenly, keys started unlocking it.

There was an amber-skinned woman with short straightened hair wearing a pink janitor's shirt and stonewashed style, fitted jeans.

"Can I help you?" she said, pulling the key out of the door.

"Yeah, I'm just waiting on my wife," I replied.

"Your wife?" the saddened baby doll face woman said, confused.

"Yes, Tracy Waters, that's my wife. Yeah, she's a counselor here for the middle school."

"Oh, okay, okay. Well, I think they're having a meeting down the hall…"

As she was talking, Tracy and Alyssa came walking down the hall. They were in a deep discussion about something. I thanked the janitor for her notification and went to meet them. The conversation faded as I approached them.

"Hi, honey. What are you doing here?" Tracy said, looking as if she was happy to see me.

Alyssa had that same peculiar look on her face that she had when she came by the house the other day.

"Here to see you," I replied, paying Alyssa no mind. "Yeah, I was gonna see if you needed a hand."

"Well, I think we've pretty much finished," Tracy said, looking at Alyssa. "We just wrapped up the teachers meeting a few minutes ago. I just need to grab my things from the room."

I turned to Alyssa. "How are you again, Alyssa?" I said with intent.

Alyssa's bleak expression turned a fake pleasant. "I'm good, Mr. Waters. We had a good meeting and I think we got some things accomplished," she said smiling.

There was something puzzling in her demeanor. Every since I told her about that event at school, she had developed a drawback in her persona.

"Tracy, I'm gonna let you guys go and I'll just talk to you tomorrow."

"Okay, Alyssa, we'll work on that forum that

you presented. Gosh, I think that's a great idea."

They said their goodbyes and Alyssa walked out the front door. I walked with Tracy to her room.

"How was work?" Tracy asked as we walked.

"Good, some of the kids started to open up a little more with this assignment. I think we're making some progress," I said, sighing relief. "What were y'all meeting about?"

Tracy opened the door to her room and walked over to her desk. "We're trying to form a program to help our middle schoolers, especially the girls. You'd be surprised by the amount of counseling I give out to just girls alone."

I grabbed Tracy's book bags and all of her belongings. Tracy's desk was cluttered with filing papers, papers with sticky note tabs with dates all over them. It's a wonder she stayed racking her brain all out into the evening.

"You keep it looking a beautiful mess don't you?" I said as we were walking out the door.

"Mess?" Tracy laughed. "This ain't mess, this is work."

We walked and talked until we made it to our cars.

"Well, are you coming straight home?" I asked.

"Only if you are," Tracy replied sarcastically.

I gave her a smile as she sat in the car. I walked over and started up my car, thinking about how much I loved Tracy – busyness and all.

# 13

WHEN I MADE it back into Jackson, I rode down the street to my house. There seemed to be something going on at Jerry's. It wasn't Thursday, the day his so-called weekly rally was held. I cruised slowly as Tracy rode along in front of me. I was curious as to what this dilemma was about.

I called Tracy on her cell and told her that I was going to stop by and see what was going on. She repeatedly insisted that I not get caught up in the conversation. I by no means was about to create a scene. My intentions were to see what the big meet-up was all about. I pulled behind the last car of the parallel line of cars on either side of the road.

As I walked toward the front of Jerry's house, there was an entourage of people gathered around in his front yard. He seemed to be standing on his porch and ranting a bunch of discrepancies as it related to Jackie, pop celebrity rubbish, and even making mention of the assignment that I had given to my class. This is what I was going to have a problem rationalizing.

Slowly easing toward the group, I noticed Jerry's eyes locking on me. His gesture turned grim and his demeanor implied detest toward me. I'm pretty sure he wondered why I was here.

"Mr. Waters," Jerry said. "I see that you decided to join us. What brought you by here?"

I smirked. "Ah, you know, just trying to see what was going on in our community. And to see if there was something that I needed to know about." I was accentuating now. I knew this meeting was all about shaking up the town.

"Hmm, well, we were just meeting to discuss some of the things that have shaken up the schools," Jerry replied. "One thing, mind you, is this talk about celebrity rigamoro and how it's affecting our students."

I frowned. "Rigamoro? I'm not quite sure I follow."

"I'm talking about this jive about stars and an assignment that was given," Jerry interjected. "You see, my son, Jason, has a friend who is a student at Lawrence Higgins High in Madison. They were talking about this whole situation of a kid hitting a teacher and what not. Also, he made mention of some assignment that was given behind it."

"Where's your son a student at?" I asked.

"Oh, he goes to a school here in Jackson," Jerry replied. "Thank goodness he's not a student over there."

I stood there and reflected on Jerry's words. At the same time, I started to wonder who made mention of the assignment I had given. There was a lot of flack behind it, but who could have told Jerry's son?

Jerry walked down the steps and into the yard,

approaching my direction slowly. "This… this celebrity bull is one of the reasons that the other students are destroying our kids. You are a teacher at Lawrence Higgins, aren't you?"

"Yes I am," I replied.

"Okay, getting caught up in the fantasy of a would-be life that projects towards nothing is a big concern."

I clenched my teeth together, wincing as I felt the muscles in my jaws tighten.

"Now, is that really what we want for our kids?" Jerry asked.

I grunted.

"Let me ask you something, Jerry. I understand that you're a computer processing manager and what not, but did you graduate college with a degree in that? Seems to me like a man of your stature would be studying computers."

Jerry cut me a grin. I guessed that he thought I was being satirical.

"No, but I did do some studying on culture and social norms," Jerry said. "I do know a thing or two about the sociological paradigms that you try to push into these kids. So this whole rodeo about the 'I am' and this assignment that you're giving those students… don't count on it too hard."

My phone vibrated in my pocket. I was willing to bet Tracy was calling to pull me away. The crowd stood there silently witnessing the indirect showdown between Jerry and me. I guessed by now they saw that Jerry was standing his ground, and so was I.

I reached in my pocket and pulled out the phone, answering it while staring at Jerry.

"Yeah, honey, I'll be there in a sec."

Jerry continued to lock eyes with mine as I talked. I hung up the phone and placed it back in my pocket. Jerry looked at me as if I had posed a threat.

"I guess that's my exit cue," I said.

"Looks like it is," Jerry beamed.

"I will say this before I go," I said. "That whole assignment that you and whoever else has problems with is not about training kids up to be an actor or an actress in Hollywood. It's to show them, Jerry, that whatever it is they desire to do when they leave that school gives them just as much of a right as any celebrity or famous person in the paparazzi world.

"It allows these students to understand that there is more to their lives than hiding behind a façade. If you had the chance to hear some of the reports and what these kids are vouching to be, then you would probably get off your high horse and beg to differ."

I could tell I was making Jerry uncomfortable.

"Jerry, I'd love to stay here and continue in the politics, but I think I'll leave that with you. How's that sound?"

Jerry inhaled deeply, brooding with an exasperated anger.

"Yeah, seeing how you have come over here and interrupted my meeting by gracing us all with your inquisitiveness to keep up with the news. I think that about sums it up. But I would like to send you away with just a word of wisdom for you to keep in mind."

I placed my hands on my hips, positioning myself for erroneous remarks and possibly a word or two of intimidation. Jerry drew in close to me.

"This town has an order we'd like to keep and a

community we'd like to protect. But if any scholastic endeavor creates chaos and possible harm to our kids by poisoning them with misguidances, then you can rest assured matters will be resolved quick, fast, and in a hurry. You think not? Try me."

I nodded. Jerry was making mention of the assignment I had given. The beauty of this whole ordeal was that everyone, from Jerry Kendell to Mr. Donnell, was missing the purpose of the assignment. I was persisting in an objective to get my class to search inside and find that inner star they had yet to become.

I turned and walked to my vehicle.

"You have a good evening, Jerry," I said.

I could tell there was a lot of tension in the air, but in due time it would all be resolved. In due time.

"Babe, I hope you aren't letting this cause you to lose focus again," Tracy said.

We had finished dinner and I was washing and drying the dishes. Tracy was sitting in a chair at our dining table. I tried to be gracious and do my part as it related to tidying the kitchen.

"I'm not losing focus, Tracy," I replied. "But I will be clear on the fact that I'm not fixing to let his threats and blackmail push me out of the way."

I placed the drying towel on the counter after I had finished.

"I can't believe this is turning into a war," I said. "One critical thinking assignment and now the whole world goes mad. From Mr. Donnell to Kendell, they're all just blowing it out of proportion."

I took a seat in the chair near her. Tracy stood up and came to take a seat on my right thigh.

"Dev, sweetheart, work is good. Helping the students find themselves is a wonderful deed, but I just don't want you to get so distracted from the things that matter the most in life. Me, for example."

I nodded as I considered her words. Maybe I was a little caught up, but I hated when something was totally misunderstood and taken to the extreme. Tracy turned and locked her arms around my neck.

"I applaud you in your efforts. I don't take any of that away from you, but… I'd like for us to think about each other sometimes."

I could feel that wind of reality sweeping over me. Tracy once again had to bring me back to grips with that thing called life. Battling against the opposition in this assignment and the sociological perspective of it all had absorbed my attention span – and quick. In my quest to help my students establish who they were, I was starting to lose focus of everyday living.

It was a fight, but one that I was willing to go to bat for. There were deeper matters that I would bring to the surface in time. Statistics showed that our kids were being warped by images and public figures in society, painting a life that was only that of smoke and mirrors. True, there were real public figures that lived genuine lives for a good cause, but there were also those who painted facades of a fairytale life. By doing so, they were causing innocent people to be deceived – young and old.

Tracy kissed me on the lips. "Don't let your life go by without you in it," she said, patting me on the chest and standing up. She turned and walked towards the room.

I stood up and walked over to our kitchen window. I leaned forward on the counter, looking through the window as if I were searching for reality – out there somewhere.

# 14

I WALKED INTO the school building the next morning. My demeanor was that of willful intent as I thought about my purpose as a teacher and how I was going to affect purpose into the hearts of my students. I just had to stay focused and not let the antagonists obstruct that path.

As I passed by Judy's office, I stopped. Dr. Spartz was standing in front of the counter that lay before Judy. Apparently, they were talking on an important matter. I turned and walked in to see what was going on.

"Hey, Devon," Dr. Spartz said, smiling.

I warmly returned the expression to him.

"Dr Spartz, what brought you by here this morning?"

Dr. Spartz tapped on his briefcase with his index finger.

"I was just here to do a follow up on the kids

from the Wise Students Wise Decisions program."

"So, are you gonna speak again?" I asked.

"No, there's a rally for them this morning at eight-thirty. They've given me time to see if I can help the students to connect with their endeavors once they leave the halls of high school."

I nodded.

"And you," Dr. Spartz said. "How's that assignment working out for you?"

I shook my head.

"You'd have to sit down and let me tell you about it. It's like watching the whole world go mad, one person at a time."

Dr. Spartz chuckled softly.

"That bad, huh?"

Judy started stacking some of the papers on her desk. I rested my book bag on the counter.

"My whole aim, Dr. Spartz, was to introduce a new light with this assignment. You know, I wanted those kids to look beyond some paparazzi image in a magazine, or on the television so that they can find that inner star in them."

Dr. Spartz raised his eyebrows.

"I only wanted them," I continued, "to know that they could be just as great as the next person. One of my students said she wants to be a registered nurse. Another one said a life coach who reaches out to women. In my opinion, a field as simple as a nurse or life coach has just as much clout as a star on the cover of a magazine.

"I don't have anything against being a celebrity, or some public figure. I just want my students to know that they can succeed as stars all across the board at whatever it is that they do. You don't have to be a rocket scientist or some big glamour something to make your contribution and attract influence."

Dr. Spartz grunted.

"Well, it sounds like you've been studying your lesson."

We both chuckled. Judy continued to sort files on her desk. I looked at the clock on the wall.

"Doc, I'd better get ready for class," I said. "Maybe we will have a chance to talk at a later time."

"Yes, yes we will," Dr. Spartz replied. "We'll have to get together for lunch sometime."

I picked up my bag and said good day to him and Judy.

"So, I've given some thought as to why some of you may feel challenged by this assignment," I said to the class. I was continuing in our discussion based on the assignment I had given them.

"During my college years we studied behind a philosopher, or sociologist for that matter. His name was Charles Cooley and he talked about something called the looking-glass self. Can anybody tell me what you think that may be?"

The students stared vaguely. I knew that wasn't something you asked a group of high school students, but I really wanted to challenge them to think.

"That theory teaches," I continued, "that an individual considers how they are viewed among other people and are judged by others. Following that, we base our character, emotions, or persona all from that one observation."

Everyone started giving offensive expressions

and glances from that statement.

"So could it be that you feel challenged to express who you really are because you think you'd be judged and examined by your fellow peers?

"Nah, you got it all wrong, teach," Anthony blurted. "It's I really just don't see the point in this assignment. Better yet, I don't see why we are takin' a simple sociology class and turnin' it all into some big philosophy classroom."

I raised an eyebrow, nodding at Anthony's observation.

"All right. Okay, do you all as a class have the same objections as Anthony to this assignment?"

No one raised their hand. I assumed it was a fear that I would offer them something a little more complex than this if they agreed.

"Go ahead, be honest. Does anyone else feel that I'm pressing this class a little too hard?"

The class still didn't dare to raise a hand. I scanned the room, observing the dumbfounded vibe that filled the air.

"Okay," I said, walking around my desk and taking a seat in my chair. "Well, class dismissed. You can go on about your day and get ready for your next class." The confusion heightened. It was still the mid part of the class period and here I was releasing the class to leave. "You're free to go. I don't want to keep you."

Meagan raised her hand.

"Mr. Waters, why are you dismissing us?"

I sat up in my chair.

"Well, it appears to me that everyone, except maybe one or two of you, are really taking this assignment seriously. So, in the interest of fairness, why waste your time?"

It appeared as if I was being cruel, but cynical was the word. I knew that I was reaching some of them, but to make my point I left the floor open for all of them.

"Mr. Waters, do you feel like you're helping us?" Meagan asked.

"No, Meagan, the question is do you feel like I'm helping you?" I said as I stood up. "From day one of this assignment, my projections and intentions have been the same. I want you as a class to really think, because when you graduate and leave here there is this thing called the real world waiting for you. If you as a person can't get the best out of your position in life because you don't know who you are, then a life out of balance can overtake you."

Silence filled the air.

"This assignment came about because one of your fellow student's activity caused a stir and no one could blatantly say what the ruckus stirred from. So everyone ranted and raved about it until the discovery was made based on a paper and a celebrity.

"My whole intent and purpose for this assignment was for you to tell me who you are and show me how the validity of who you are holds just as much weight as anyone on the big screen. Public figures and superstars rise up all the time, but I want you to believe that regardless of what it is you desire to attain in life, it can be just as grand as other things and people that we hold in high esteem."

I went and stood in front of Anthony's desk.

"Anthony's right," I said, looking down at him.

"This is a sociology class and we study the routine of social topics of the semester. But our current topic of study just happens to be dealing with the self. Why not take and incorporate the dilemma talked about into it?"

Meagan raised her hand again.

"Mr. Waters, may I?" she said, nudging the paper on her desk in front of her.

I gave her a nod of courtesy, encouraging her to proceed. Meagan picked up her paper.

"The I Am Assignment. When I first started this assignment, I thought it was a big waste of time, but I knew that it was something that I had to do so I might as well get it over with."

I chuckled softly.

"When considering who I am," Meagan continued, "I wondered if I could call myself anything, then what would it be? I would have to say that I am a registered nurse put on this earth to help as many people who may be disabled or sick as I can. This desire stirred in me because two years ago…"

Meagan started to choke and get teary eyed.

"Two years ago, my mother died of breast cancer and I vowed to save…"

The cry within unleashed. I walked over to Meagan's desk, placing a hand on her shoulder. The class became startled, stunning at the seriousness of what Meagan said. Everyone saw the impact of this assignment. Even Anthony in his tough guy façade had to let his guard down and see the potential of the assignment.

"You see, that's how you know when a thing has become real to you," I said. "I'm not trying to get you to write something that you think will impress. I want this work to become real to you. The potential to do some big things is in you. That's what I want you to see."

The bell finally rang after all that discussion and explanation, bringing today's class to an end. I thought the power of what I had charged these students with would pay off in the end.

"Meagan, can I speak to you for just a minute?" I said to her as she readied to walk through the door. Meagan held her books close to her chest.

"Yeah, Mr. Waters."

I walked to her and placed a hand on her shoulder.

"I know it took a lot of courage to do what you did, but I am so proud of you."

Meagan grinned. "Thank you."

I smiled back.

"Listen, you hold to this assignment. I believe you will make a brilliant nurse."

I gave her a pat on the shoulder and let her go. In the midst of all the misunderstandings and opposition, I knew that I would help to change at least one person's perspective. Meagan proved that.

# 15

"SO SHE PRACTICALLY broke down in the classroom," I said to Tracy. Tracy was fixing dinner.

I was telling her about today's class experience.

"Well, it looks like you may be finally reaching them," Tracy said.

"Yeah, and one of the students really was starting to lose faith in this project." I was making reference to Anthony. "So, if we press in a little more I think we may finally reach them, and also make a statement to the school administration as well."

I started walking toward the living room.

"Did you need me to help you with something, honey?" I said as I stopped in my tracks.

Tracy laid the dish towel on the cabinet.

"Nah. Well, you can take this trash bag out."

I rounded up the bag and tied it up, then I walked through the side door and out to the trash can. As I was walking outside, I saw Jerry across the street talking to a neighbor from the porch. He talked to her fervently, presenting her with a brochure. He looked like a spokesman for Jehovah's Witness. I stood there by the can, looking on.

Jerry handed her the brochure and shook her hand. I started to get a feeling of uneasiness. I started to wonder if this was another one of his pranks to try to win someone over to his side. He turned to leave and gave me a wave as he neared his truck.

"How are you?" Jerry yelled out.

"Fine," I replied. "What, are you passing out flyers?"

"Something like that," Jerry replied. He walked across the street toward my direction.

*Brace yourself for the conflict.*

I told myself as he came toward me with a few of the brochures in his hand.

"Here you go. You can have one, too."

It was a little folded brochure with information on each side. As I looked it over, I saw that the theme was on the subject of anti-celebrity. It gave tips on how to keep the youth from being ruined, so to speak. Now it was good that he was directing for a good cause to help teens and those in our community, but I knew that the opposition against public figures and an assault against the essay I had given was the primary target. The students were used as the cover up. Really, the shot was being taken at me.

"Oh, it's just some information to help encourage parents and the community to help our kids," Jerry said. "We have to try to take our students back."

"Why are you doing this, Jerry?"

Jerry frowned. "You know that the only reason you're into this whole whim is because of that assignment that I presented."

"Well, sir, call it what you will," Jerry said. "But, I'm trying to help draw this community together."

"No you're not," I exclaimed. "What you really want is a war. A war that puts the community and the school against me. You see me trying to help to bring out the best in these students. But, because you're so brainwashed with all these antics you feel that I'm trying to steer them in the wrong direction."

"Brainwashed? If anyone here is brainwashed, Devon, it's you. Talking all this jive to these kids about a star in them; you really want to protect this celebrity bull…"

"I'm not trying to protect nothing," I said fervently. "These kids live in a world where social status has misdirected them, and it has caused them to lose identity of who they are. Not just the students, but adults too. You may have lost your identity, as well."

Jerry pointed a finger and started a smart-mouth comeback when Tracy walked out through the door.

"Is everything all right out here?" Tracy asked.

"Yeah, is everything all right out here, Jerry?" I said, looking at him with intent.

Jerry smirked. "Yeah, Mrs. Waters, your husband and I were just talking."

There was a stare down between Jerry and me. I wanted to put him on the spot for his shenanigans just as bad as he wanted to slam me.

Jerry walked backwards slowly.

"You people have a pleasant evening."

He then turned and walked across the street to his truck. I sighed, wiping my face with both hands.

"Devon, what's going on out here?" Tracy

asked.

I grunted.

"Well, sweetheart, I was taking this trash out," I said, holding the bag still. "And I saw him across the street talking with the neighbor. He walked to his truck with a hand full of brochures and I made an inquiry of them."

Tracy slanted her head to the left, twisting her lips.

"And he came over here," I continued, "carrying those brochures."

Tracy took the brochure from my hand and looked over it.

"So he starts giving me this speech about taking back the community and the kids and how this celebrity jive is ruining the youth and…"

"Devon, why do you keep letting this guy get to you?" Tracy asked. "Honey, you just gotta know that if it's working for you, and the school hasn't got you, then help the ones that will let you help them."

"But, that's just it, Tracy," I exclaimed. "People like Jerry Kendell just won't let it down. He's just gonna keep prying and prying until he can win this whole town to his side."

"Well, you can't win 'em all," Tracy cried out, throwing up both hands in the air. "You win some, you lose some, but that's the way the game goes. You can't win the favor of everybody. As long as you know that what you're doing is helping at least one person, then you can rest your hat on the banister of time knowing that you, Devon Waters, you changed one person's life."

I inhaled deeply. As much as my blood boiled

within me, what Tracy said made sense.

"I'm going back inside," Tracy said, walking to the side door. "Think about it."

She went back in and I stood there still hanging on to the loops of the trash bag. I looked across the street and down our block. As bad as I wanted to win the whole city, I knew that everyone wasn't going to follow me. However, to the ones that did I was certain that they would know I left a mark. That was one thing that you could be sure about.

# 16

"SO THIS GUY just keeps going on and on," I said to Darby. It was the weekend and I went by his coffee shop Saturday morning.

When I left the house, Tracy was still in bed. My mind with its agitations stirred like a madman. Plus, I hadn't been by Darby's in a while. If there was chatter I needed to relieve, then he was the one for it. Darby was always open to hear my school drama.

"Well, you can't let 'em get you down, Dev," Darby said, wiping the granite countertop with a rag. "You know you gonna always have somebody try to bring you down. You just gotta stay focused,"

"Yeah, you sound like Tracy now," I jeered. "She keeps telling me the same thing. I guess I just hate to see the bad guys win, if that makes any sense."

Darby chuckled. "Oh, come on now. The guy can't be all that bad."

I shrugged. We sat there and talked for a little while longer before I decided to get up and head out. My coffee break moment with Darby helped to calm my anguish and relax me. Now I felt like I could go on about my day, and hope that nothing else drastic would be made of it.

I headed back home. My guess was that Tracy was awake by now, seeing that it was ten minutes after nine. I turned in the driveway of the house and walked out to the front. I looked at the hedges and noticed that it was time to trim them.

Between school time and home life, my life stayed pretty busy. That was one of the joys of being a teacher; you never had to worry about finding something to do outside of class work. Tracy's schedule and mine stayed full. I unlocked the door and went inside. Tracy was sitting at the table looking through a magazine.

"Hey," she said, looking up from her reading. "Where you been? I got up and you weren't there."

"Oh, I went down to Darby's," I replied. "I was awake early so I decided to go out for coffee." I sat down in a chair next to her, flinging the keys on the table. "What you reading?"

"This was a magazine that came in the mail," Tracy replied. "It was one I subscribed to. You look tired, are you okay?"

"Me? Yeah," I said, slumping forward with my elbows on my knees. "Yeah, just my mind going, you know."

Tracy closed her magazine and walked to me, taking a seat on my right thigh. She placed her arm around my neck.

"Why don't we go out this evening?" Tracy said. "It's the weekend we're away from work, why don't the two of us just go out?"

I turned my head and looked at her.

"That sounds like a good idea," I said. "Seems like I need something to get my mind off of the agitations and what not."

Tracy stood up. "Yeah, let's go. I think that'll be good for the both of us."

The work flow was getting the best of me. I think some time to get away would be just the thing that I needed.

Later that evening, Tracy and I went to a dine-and-dance café. La Viva Cabana, a café up in north Jackson, was a place for the grown and sexy. Tracy and I never spent much time getting acquainted with each other. She was right; we were so caught up in work that I never spent the time connecting with her. That was a sad reality, but it was true.

The La Viva Cabana was a two-stored affair with an upstairs usually reserved for special events and parties. Downstairs was the main floor where many of the patrons frequented. The color contour was white, chocolate, and ebony. The white tablecloth on the tables were composed of a black saxophone shaped ornament and silverware wrapped in black napkins.

"You know, honey, I'm really glad we had a chance to do this," I said as Tracy and I dined at our table. "I know we're busy all through the week, but I really feel that this gives me more time with you."

Tracy smiled, holding her fork as she chewed. "See, I told you that this would hit the spot. And, you're right we don't spend much time getting to know each other."

I reached across the table and placed my hand on hers.

"Trace, I know we've only been married for five years, but that is still no reason for me to be treating this as if we're newlyweds. I do want to make an impact, don't get me wrong about that. But, I also want to be the husband that you knew when we first married."

Tracy gave a look of courtesy. "You know, I'm really glad to hear you say that. I don't ever, ever want to take from you being a strong man and teacher. Devon, what you are doing to reach out to these students is phenomenal. I just don't want you to lose yourself, or us for that matter."

I stared away in a reverie as a song played through the stereo. Tracy gave a puzzled look, as well.

"Hey, is that our song?" I asked.

It was the song that Tracy and I danced to at our wedding.

"I think it is," Tracy replied.

I stood up and walked around the table, extending my hand. "May I have this dance?"

Tracy smiled, blushing. "Are you sure about that?"

"Positive," I replied with charm.

Tracy pushed back her chair as I took her by the hand. We walked out onto the open floor where other couples slow danced, mixed, and mingled. We danced and enamored ourselves with memories from back when.

As we moved and grooved slowly, Tracy stopped. We stared into each other's eyes as the affection rekindled.

"I love you," Tracy said.

I leaned forward and kissed the woman who had been with me through thick and thin, good and the not so good, but most importantly I kissed the one who would share in the countenance of us both shaping the world for the better.

"I love you too, babe," I replied. "From now until infinity."

# 17

I WALKED INTO the teacher's lounge Monday morning to make some copies for my first period class. There were several other teachers in there as well. Mrs. Ettore, the Spanish teacher, was at the copier then and I went and stood behind her. There were two teachers standing in the corner drinking coffee and gossiping. That was usually the case in the teacher's lounge, and the reason why I kept my trips there at a minimum.

While I stood waiting on Mrs. Ettore to finish, Greg Maxwell came walking through the door. I hadn't run into him since our clash in the parking lot several days ago. He was holding a manila folder under his arm as he walked toward my direction.

"Devon, how are you this morning?" Greg said.

"Good, Greg, how's Biology going for you?" I said, directing our conversation to that end to avoid any trivial talk or conflict.

"Biology's good. Yeah, it's going real good."

Mrs. Ettore gathered up her copies and turned

to leave, almost running into me.

"So, I heard that kid made it to the juvenile center?"

I placed my paper on the copy machine and punched in the amount of copies that I needed and the start button.

"Why are you telling me?" I said.

"Well, they said that he could be suspended from school for a while for what he did. Man, that's gotta be tough."

I knew where this innuendo was going, and who it was being lashed at. Greg gave that sympathetic tone in his speech, but a sound of victory hid beneath it. He was probably glad to hear that Jackie was serving time there.

"Yeah, they gave him a little time," I replied. "But it's all good, though. Everyone gets off of the path every now and then." My copies had finished printing. "Well, I'd love to stand here and chat, but I have a first period class full of star students and we have a project to complete this week."

Greg smirked. I left him standing there and walked to the door.

"Star students, huh?" Greg said.

I turned around to him, standing at the door. "Yeah, like I said… star students. Something wrong with that?"

"No, it's just that's the first time I've heard a teacher use that."

Greg's sarcasm was increasing. His comments were intended to make a mockery of me.

"Just hang around," I replied. "You may hear some more phrases that you never heard a teacher use."

I left out of the room on that. I had more important matters to concern myself with.

"Okay, okay. So listen," I said to the class. "Your papers are due this Friday. You should be at the typing stage by now and nearing to finish."

Anthony raised his hand. "Mr. Waters, did you check out that flyer that some guy was handin' out?"

"Flyer?" I replied. "What are you talking about?"

"This guy is doing a rally that promotes the growth of teens by weeding out talk of brainwashing them with celebrities and public figures."

I frowned. "Weeding out talk of celebrities?"

"Yeah," Anthony replied. "Well, that's not exactly how the flyer says it, but that's the whole point. I think it talks about how the corruption of public figures have polluted the teen's mind. Like a deal against celebrities and what not."

I placed the manila folder I was holding on the edge of my desk. I reckoned this slander could only be coming from one person. I was willing to bet it was the same person who handed out that brochure to my neighbor across the street.

"Tell me, Anthony, where did you see this flyer?" I said.

"In the window at Jona's Grill & Fixin's around the corner," Anthony replied. "I saw it this morning when I got me somethin' for breakfast."

I wanted to share my misery to the class of my adversary along this journey, but it wouldn't be in my best interest to do so. I wanted them to know the name of the jackal whose mind was oblivious to what I wanted to accomplish with this assignment. My purpose was to use this assignment in order for the students to search inside for their greater selves and become the star people they were intended to be. Jerry Kendell wanted to dismiss everything in hopes that he could lull the students' minds from dreaming in order to keep them trapped in a box of complacency.

"I tell you what," I said. "Why don't you just spend these last few days focusing on completing this assignment and see, after it's all said and done, if it helps you to move forward toward your future?"

Meagan raised her hand. "Mr. Waters, do you really think that once we finish this we would have accomplished anything?"

"Well, I'll flip it. Do you really feel that you will have accomplished anything?"

"I mean, yeah I feel like I would have," Meagan replied. "But it's trying to convince everyone else that we achieved something. Like all the teachers, or whatever, are probably totally against what we're doing so they're the ones we really gotta convince."

I folded my arms.

"What makes you think you gotta convince them?" I asked, puzzled.

"I mean, who else believes in this stuff?" Meagan replied wryly, smacking on her gum. "This is probably the only class in the entire high school giving an assignment that is actually concentrating on a student's dream life after they leave this place."

Listening to Meagan's speech, you would think that she was some ditzy blonde with a pretty face, but the way she spoke was actually convincing me that she was taking this assignment to heart.

"Hmm. So… what do you propose?" I asked.

"I say we read the papers to the school board," Anthony interrupted. "They're probably the ones we gotta convince anyway."

"What are you trying to convince?" I said, challenging them to think about what they were asking.

"Try to convince everybody that Jackie's reaction was done out of probable cause," Anthony said. "Mr. Waters, he was doin' an assignment and, for whatever the teacher said, he popped him because the teacher probably said somethin' smart-mouth."

"But that's just it, Anthony," I said, cutting him off. "You have to give all your heart to this assignment. This I Am assignment isn't just about writing something to prove someone wrong. This is about writing with sincere, heartfelt, truthful words and letting those who are in positions of authority see that you all are not just some group of students taking classes just to be done with school.

"Life does go on after you graduate, but you have to put some mind behind the muscle, and in a sense show the board or whoever why they should grant Jackie liberty and let him come back."

"Well, alls I gotta say is," Meagan said. "If I make my point, and I know I gave my all, they gonna have to give us some respect."

The bell rang and everyone gathered their things.

"Okay, this is deadline time," I said. "The due date for this assignment is rapidly approaching. Let's finish this strong."

Everyone exited the room. I took a seat in my chair, reclining as I thought on today's class. I began to think that it had taken the crunch time and the press for time of this assignment to open these students' eyes. It's as if this was narrowed down to the final hour, and this moment was going to either make them or break them.

# 18

WHEN I GOT back into Jackson, I stopped by Walgreens off of Mississippi Avenue to pick up some pictures. Tracy said that she would be late getting home so she asked me if I would stop by and pick them up. She said that they had a teachers meeting after school.

As I walked to the entrance, I saw a flyer taped to the window next to it.

"Open our students' minds and weed out the distractions," I said, reading the sign.

I wonder if this was the same flyer that Anthony was talking about. It amazed me how Jerry was on a wildfire run to try to stop what I was doing. What really made me get the notion was how this man was posting flyers all the way up in Madison where I taught.

I read on the flyer where Jerry was holding a rally on Wednesday evening at the city park. I knew that Jerry's intentions weren't about drawing the community together to help our students. No, this was a war to gain the support of others.

Jerry believed that my assignment was resulting in "manipulating" the teens with some imagery of celebrity flamboyance. However, that was far from the truth.

My sole intent with the I Am assignment was to show that my class didn't have to look to the celebrities of today's world in order gain attention from others. The big screen wasn't the only place to get notoriety. If they desired to be a physician, accountant, or marketing research analyst then that should gain them the same credence that a Hollywood star received.

I walked inside and over to the photo section. The clerk was checking out a patron. I stood in line behind them and waited my turn. Shaking the clerk's hand, the man turned around and tension filled the air. My eyes locked with his and it was as if I was standing toe to toe with an adversary.

"Oh, well… hello, Devon," Jerry Kendell said, extending his hand.

I stared at his hand and then at him, looking him in the eyes.

"So, picking up more material to add to your demise?" I said.

Jerry sneered. "Demise? Now, I wouldn't say that. And, by the way… what does that supposed to mean?"

"It means I see what you're doing," I replied. "Trying to polish everything up in a help the teens rally, but in reality you wanna take shots at what I'm doing. And you need a community of people to feed that energy."

"I don't know what you're talking about," Jerry

said.

"You know exactly what I'm talking about," I replied fervently. "You think that I'm deceiving these kids with celebrity bravado, but you're sadly mistaken and missing the whole purpose of the assignment I've given."

The male clerk behind the counter stood there, waiting patiently for me to step forward. I walked to the counter and requested the pictures.

"I'm here to pick up photos for Tracy Waters," I said to the man, keeping my eyes locked on Jerry.

The clerk stepped aside and searched through the orders for Tracy's.

"Listen, Devon, I keep hearing you talk about the assignment and the students. I could care less about what it is that you're doing. I…" Jerry started chuckling. "I, on the other hand, am about bringing clarity to matters."

"Clarity?" I snapped. "Please tell me through all these antics and stretching of the truth that you don't believe that you're bringing clarity?"

Jerry twisted his lip, frowning with frustration.

"Jerry, all I gotta say is this. Just pray your efforts don't backfire when this is all said and done."

"And you," Jerry replied, pointing a finger, "better hope all you're teaching and convincing doesn't prove to be utter folly."

I leaned on the counter as I held my countenance at Jerry. The clerk walked to the counter with the pictures and I paid for them. As I walked away from the counter, so did Jerry.

"Well, in the words of battle," Jerry said. "May the best man win."

He walked on out the door.

He could say what he wanted. I didn't care if I was in this all alone, because I believed in my students. And not only did I believe in them, but I believed that they had a winning chance.

"I assure you it's not like that," I said, sitting on the side of my bed with the phone to my ear.

I was on the phone with the principal, Mr. Donnell. He was talking to me about the assignment. It seemed to have caused a stir.

"You too... well, I think it's one thing for everyone to have an opinion, and that's what I'm trying to say, Mr. Donnell, Jerry Kendell is stretching his point and opinion."

Mr. Donnell had seen a flyer posted on the wall at the same restaurant Anthony had. It was enough that Jerry was masquerading around town here in Jackson, but he was carrying his efforts up to Madison. That was a bit much.

Tracy came out of the bathroom drying her wet hair with a towel. She was so gorgeous in my eyes, and the sight of her caused me to lose focus on the phone with Mr. Donnell.

"Okay, like I said, Mr. Donnell, we're almost finished with this assignment, and then we can move from there."

Tracy stood in front of me, luring me in with her eyes. She then crawled in the bed behind me, and kneeled as she wrapped her arms my neck and laid her head on my shoulder. I knew this was an indication that I had been on the phone long enough.

I turned to her and gave her a kiss.

"Okay, Mr. Donnell it's getting late in the evening. A few more days, that's all. Then you can see if all my efforts were false."

We wrapped up our phone conversation, and then I hung up the phone. It was 9:37 on the clock by my bed stand. Jerry was giving me a fight, but I was certain that he would see that I wasn't about to back down.

I laid over on the bed and Tracy rested on top of me with her arms folded where she could rest her head.

"Boy, they are giving you a run for your money," Tracy said.

"Ain't they?" I replied. "That's all right though, when it's all said and done that's all that matters."

Tracy grunted. She rolled off of me and to her side of the bed.

"So, have you heard anything else from Alyssa?" I asked.

Tracy took her earrings off. "Yeah, I mean she's helping me with this young adult awareness program for the girls at school."

That's not what I was insinuating to her. There was something strange about Alyssa, and every since the day I first met her I wanted to keep an eye on her.

"Trace, don't you think there's something strange about her? I mean, the day I first met her and told her about that deal with Mr. Buckley at school she's seemed kinda – weird."

"Honey, don't pay that no mind," Tracy replied. "Alyssa's someone that you have to just know how to take. She's as sweet as can be, and you just have to know how to accept her."

I knew how to accept her, all right. I had to keep her under surveillance from a distance. She may have been nice as she could be, but the enigma of her just didn't sit well with me.

We turned out the lights and I drew in close to Tracy, holding her in my arms as we lay there.

"I was thinking," Tracy said softly. "That when this is all over with, you know this project with your class and my working with the girls at school, we could… take that vacation, you know. Go somewhere far away."

I thought about what Tracy said. I really needed to get away with my wife, seeing how we were so engulfed in work.

"Well, what'd you have in mind?" I asked.

"Doesn't matter," Tracy replied. "Just somewhere that doesn't involve paperwork, students, or co-workers."

I chuckled.

"Yeah, I hear that. Hmm… well, I tell you what. Just tell me where you wanna go, and I'll do everything to make it happen. I promise."

Tracy turned over and faced me. "That's why I love you."

And I meant that. At this level, I would hang the moon for Tracy just to see her happy. No matter what came or went, I would see to it that I would fulfill that promise. And you could take that to the bank.

# 19

I ARRIVED AT the school early the next morning. I had some work that I wanted to get done before my first period class started. As I entered the building, I saw Mr. Buckley getting ready to walk into the secretary's office.

"Mr. Buckley," I said, flagging his attention before he walked in.

"Well, good morning, Mr. Waters," he said with a strong southern accent. "How are you?"

"I'm good, sir," I replied. "Listen, do you have a minute? I need to ask you something."

Mr. Buckley drew his stack of manila folders to his chest. "Sure, what can I help you with?"

"I'm pretty sure you've heard about the rave on the assignment I've given to my first period class."

Mr. Buckley nodded, intrigued.

"Now, you know I'm not the type for confrontation," I continued, "I believe in a good course of study that is meant to bring out the best in an individual.

"What Jackie Rollins did to you I totally disagree with, but I have to ask you, sir… what did you say to him that caused him to react the way he did? I mean, something must have been said."

I presented myself to Mr. Buckley in a subtle manner, but really I knew he had said something to Jackie that caused him to take a swing.

"Mr. Waters, I'll say it like this. Jackie stood up in class and did his report. I gave my thoughts and sentiments about it, as I did to all the other students that read their essays. I critiqued him on things that he could add whenever he wrote his next paper, and he rambled on and on about how he felt about the matter. And…"

The door to the office flew open.

"Mr. Buckley, I have those files on my desk," Jillian Rivers, the freshman English teacher said. "I know you had asked me about them so I'm kind of in a hurry before class starts. Do you mind coming to take a look at them?"

Mr. Buckley scrambled with the folders in his hand. "Yes, Jillian let me turn in these reports to the office right quick and I'll be right down there."

Jillian walked expeditiously down the hall. Mr. Buckley pulled the door handle to the office open. "Mr. Waters, you and I could go on and on with this, but I really need to do this and get down there to help her."

"Okay, but Mr. Buckley…" I started.

"Time, Mr. Waters, time," Mr. Buckley said, rushing into the office.

I stood there wondering if he would have enlightened me about what Jackie said to him when they were out in the hallway. That also made me wonder what was said in the comments Mr. Buckley gave regarding Jackie's report.

The comments of critique may have been what were needed to write the "perfect paper" for the class, but that wasn't what I wanted to know. It was what was discussed while out in the hallway that really mattered.

"Okay, so I know you've been asking," I said to my first period class. "What will we gain after this assignment, after all the lessons on social issues and so forth, what will this do for me? What will it do for Jackie? Well… someone wanna tell me what they think it will do?"

I scanned the room, anticipating an answer. Nathan raised his hand.

"Yes, Nathan."

"Uh, I… I hope for our sake that justice will prevail, first of all. Maybe the school will see that we're not just a bunch of students here taking up space."

"And yeah, maybe stop thinkin' all of us is the same," Anthony interrupted.

Nathan nodded slightly with a face of cowardice.

"We started this whole lesson off with talkin' about individuality," Anthony continued, "and how social independence has been shut down for so long. Then we started talkin' this talk about I Am, and celebrity and all that."

"And what has that done for you?" I shrieked with both hands in the air. "Where do you stand now after all of this time?"

Anthony pondered that question. "Ha, where do I stand? I'll tell you where I stand. I still stand wonderin' if after all this will we win… or will we perish, Mr. Waters?"

I thought about the answer that Anthony had given. I turned and walked around behind my desk, leaning forward on it with both fist.

"Personally, I believe that the strength of this assignment is going to be determined by the sincerity and heartfelt effort put into it. Again, I say you can do the time, put in the work just to skate through. But, what are you gonna do when an opportunity is given, or presented to you by a member of the administrative school system that allows you to vouch for your fellow student? Are you gonna read some paper that hardly carries the weight of salt that's put in it?"

I was at a tipping point.

"This is the last straw. You all are in the final round and what you say or what you mean is what's going to determine if you've really passed the test. The test of whether my story gives me a voice, or if it helps me intervene for a fellow student and friend. Can I really answer the mystery of what was said that pushed my fellow student, Jackie, to retaliate in the manner that he did?"

A knock came at the door. It was Mr. Phillips, the Algebra teacher.

"Hey, Devon, can I see you in the hall for just a moment?" Mr. Phillips said, poking his head into the classroom. I sat the marker I held on my desk and walked into the hall.

I closed the door behind me. "Yes, Mr. Phillips, how can I help you?"

Mr. Phillips was a short pudgy man. He looked to be in his late forties or early fifties. He stood there with his hands in the pockets of his khaki pants.

"I'm pretty sure you're familiar with this whole ordeal behind this anti-celebrity battle and so forth, Devon? Well... I think you might want to call a truce."

Truce? Surely he didn't think that I was going to back down this close to the end. And it amazed me that he would come down to talk about this while I'm having a critical thinking discussion with my class.

"Excuse me?" I said.

"Mr. Waters, all of my students, all of my classes, are taking this pretty seriously. The talk about an assignment that was given in a class, I mean it's all just insane. And this riot of this so called anti-celebrity battle...it's just too much."

"Okay, Mr. Phillips, first of all," I said. "I don't know the whole of this with your classes and all, but whatever this so called battle that you're talking about is, I'm sorry to say that you're sadly mistaken. I'm doing an assignment in one of my classes based on a study we're doing. Now this anti-celebrity jargon you're talking about, you're gonna have to talk to the person who is heading up that disturbance."

I knew who was causing the commotion. I wasn't about to go into a dissertation with Mr. Phillips about it. I was determined to finish that class project if I had to put everything on the line. I had to show Jerry Kendell and any other obstructionist that there was more to this course of study than some lousy assignment to try to start a war.

"I sure hope you know what you've gotten yourself into, Mr. Waters," Mr. Phillips said. "For your sake, and that of your class."

I winced a glare.

"Time will tell," I replied.

I turned and walked back into the classroom. At this point it was all or nothing, and pretty soon everyone would find that out.

# 20

I SAT ON the couch later that evening watching an interview on CNN. There was a man named Cornell Jones being interviewed about his political and social views of the world. He had written a bestselling book titled *Epic View and Epic You: profiles from the world we live in.* He was a philosopher with a doctorate degree in philosophy. He spoke of how society lived predominantly in misinterpreted paradigms that alter the true self. That was an interesting point.

Tracy hadn't made it home yet. Usually she would notify me if she was going to be late. I assumed that she was still bogged in school work.

I heard the sound of keys and ruckus plop down on the counter in the kitchen behind me. I turned around. It was Tracy

"Hey, babe, you scared me," I said.

Tracy had a troubled expression on her face. She walked to the couch and sat on the coffee table in front of me. She took me by the hands.

"What's wrong?" I asked.

Tracy tilted her head to the side, shaking it slowly. "You… you remember Alyssa that we talked about?"

"Of course I do," I replied remorsefully.

"Well, we were working on a project that we had been doing all week for a group of girls at the school. We talked and chattered randomly as we worked and talked about several things that we could do to better reach these girls. Anyway, we somehow got on the subject about what happened at your school and that incident with the kid who hit the teacher."

The muscles in my arm flinched, shuddering at the thought of that.

"So we went on and on with that, and she told me something that shocked my world."

And that last statement about the kid and the student was shocking my world. Now it was serious. I braced myself for the worse and prepared myself for possibly the sum of my fears. Tracy continued to look troubled as she shook her head slowly.

"Baby, what is it?" I asked. "What'd she say?"

Tracy raised her head slowly and looked me in the eyes with dread. "She said… she said that teacher, Mr. Buckley, that Jackie hit… was her uncle."

My heart dropped, feeling as if it was clashing through several floors of glass. Everything in my conscience, and really everything in my being, reminded me of the suspicion I had about Alyssa.

"Wa-wa-wait a minute," I stuttered. "You mean Mr. Buckley is Alyssa's uncle?"

"Yeah, and I guess the shock of it all just had

her startled."

Which would be the reason why she looked at me the way she did that day.

"Well, how is she now?" I asked. "What'd she say?"

"She says that she doesn't know what to think," Tracy replied, squeezing my hand slightly. "I mean, she said that something had to either have been said or done to trigger that whole incident."

"I'll tell you what it is," I exclaimed, standing up and releasing Tracy's hand. "That kid was inspired by something that occurred and it really touched him. But I'm willing to bet that Mr. Buckley counted it as foolish and expressed his opinion to the point that Jackie hit him, plain and simple."

Tracy stood up and walked toward the kitchen. "Whatever it is I'll be glad when it's all over. This mess has gone on long enough."

"I know it has," I replied, looking out of my patio door. I noticed that a pot of my petunias was dying. I walked to the glass door.

I opened the door and walked out on the patio. I kneeled down and picked up the pot. I turned a leaf on the plant, pitying the shriveled leaves.

"Ain't that something," I said. "Letting these flowers die."

I sat the pot down and stood up. Tracy was standing behind me. She dashed her weight at me, wrapping my waist with her arms.

"Have you decided on that vacation yet?" I asked, turning around.

Tracy looked me in the eyes. "I was thinking that we'd go to Cozumel. You know, it's nice this time of year."

It was early spring, so the weather would be perfect for sunny skies and pretty water. Come to think of it, anything would be paradise compared to the catastrophe of the past week or so.

"Well, it's spring now," I said. "Do you wanna do spring break?"

Tracy pondered it as she glanced up at the ceiling. "We might could pull it for spring break. But then, we could do it after school is out, or…"

We both laughed simultaneously.

"Listen," I said. "I tell you what, how about I get through with this whole assignment ordeal and we call a truce then?"

Tracy smiled, laying her head to the side.

"Deal."

I held Tracy close, hugging her and reflecting on how this was a deal that would do us good. Not just good, but all the good.

# 21

I WALKED INTO the school building the next morning. The time and due date for the class's assignment was dwindling away.

"Mr. Waters?"

I stopped in mid stride and turned. It was Mr. Donnell, the principal.

"Mr. Donnell, how are you?"

He walked toward me with a snarled grin plastered on his face.

"Mr. Waters, I'm here to draw a line."

I frowned. "Excuse me?"

"This whole school paper and assignment, or whatever, is causing a lot of grievances and disturbance to Lawrence Higgins High. And, as a principal, I gotta pull the plug."

"Are you serious?" I said enraged. "Mr. Donnell, we are a few days away from the final for this project. Now, you can't expect for me, or the students for that matter, to have worked hard and long, busting our tails only to tell me to drop it all now."

"But that's what you're missing, Devon," Mr. Donnell exclaimed. "It seems the longer I let you linger with this, the more trouble that gets stirred."

I sat my book bag down on the hall floor.

"Mr. Donnell," I said, clasping both hands together. "I know you want to end this now, but I'll make a deal with you. How about Friday morning in the school auditorium I let my students present to you? What if you get the members of the school board together and you and the board be the judge of whether I have wasted my time or not?"

"You can't be serious, Devon," Mr. Donnell replied. "Do you really think it's that serious to where I need to get the board involved? I mean, Devon, these people have busy schedules and…"

"And they probably know the ruckus that's been going on," I added. "And they've probably heard about the whole of it, too. So… so why don't we call a vote? If after the students read and give their presentations and the board hold it in favor, we win. If the board feels that I've wasted time and have ruined these students' minds by brainwashing them, then I lose my position and you find someone else to replace me?"

Mr. Donnell folded his arms, looking perplexed. "Do you know what you're asking? Putting your job on the line?"

I held my chin up in confidence.

"Winner takes all," I replied. "It's all or nothing. I as a teacher win, or I as a teacher perish."

Mr. Donnell rationalized my proposition in his mind, pacing side to side.

"Devon, do you really know what you're asking me to do?" Mr. Donnell said. "Devon, you are risking your career all for the sake of an assignment."

I chuckled softly.

"Mr. Donnell, I am absolute in what I'm asking. You see, you have some who think that I'm trying to vouch for a celebrity or public figure. You have some who think that I am trying to defend the music industry and all that, but that's not the case."

Mr. Donnell raised an eyebrow.

"This assignment," I continued, "is bigger than defending a celebrity. This assignment is about allowing this class to allow that star person inside them to come out, a star beyond the big screen and red carpet."

"All right," Mr. Donnell said. "If you're so sure about this that you would risk your position as a teacher… I say… deal. I'll give you the opportunity to plea your case if I can get members of the board together here on Friday morning."

That was music to my ears. I at least had a chance at liberty, and now my students would have to exert earnestness, seeing that the job of their teacher was at stake.

"Okay, everybody listen up," I said to my first period class as we started for the morning. "As you know the assignment is due on Friday, and I really hope that you all have put your best into it."

"Mr. Waters, are we gonna get like a gold medal or something when this assignment is over?" Meagan said, sarcastically.

The class laughed at the thought of that idea.

"That's funny, Meg, but I have something a little better to offer," I said. The class looked at me with anticipation. "Class, Friday morning you all are going to present your assignment, but you're not just gonna stand before the class and read it."

The class twisted their faces, puzzled.

"You're gonna stand before the members of the school board."

"What!" Meagan exclaimed.

"Mr. Waters, you can't be serious?" Anthony added.

"Listen, this whole assignment came about because you were all ticked off by Jackie's situation. So to even things, I presented you with an assignment in conjunction with the lesson we were studying and told you that this could maybe cause some retribution in the case of Jackie verses Mr. Buckley."

"But, Mr. Waters, we didn't think you were serious about us and the board," Anthony said. "Do you really think we have a chance against them?"

I plopped the tablet I held onto my desk.

"What do you think I have been teaching you?" I cried. "Do you think I have been doing this just so that we could have a good little classroom discussion?"

A sense of direct intent fell on the class.

"Before we started this lesson we talked about individuality, and furthered it with social individualism. Well, the favor of unfairness brooded and to equalize all the discrepancies I presented to you as a class an assignment. Because your fellow classmate did a report on a celebrity who did something for a good cause, he ran into controversy with a teacher.

"I said to you that if you feel like things were out of line, then maybe if you did this assignment it would give you a voice." Everyone was in a daze of critical thinking. "Jackie did a report over a celebrity, so

I asked you to tell the world who you are. What is your arena of stardom and area of expertise? If you had that same kind of notoriety that the celebrity Jackie did in his essay had, what area would be attributed to you? What would the script read if you were displayed in the celebrity world?"

My speech and presentation was beginning to sink in. I had exerted many efforts to make sure that my class would do what they needed to in order to be known and heard. If my efforts for this mission were not complete, then we as a whole would have wasted our class time.

"Class, you all have to give your best in this report. I know that it's in you… and you all have to make sure that Friday morning you exert the best that you have. Because… because if you as a class don't I… I as your teacher could be replaced."

"Replaced?" Anthony exclaimed. "What you talkin' about, Mr. Waters?"

"The principal, Mr. Donnell, wants to shut down this whole assignment," I replied, holding up my right hand to signal peace. "I negotiated with him and asked if he would give you all a chance to read your essays before members of the school board."

Terror filled the air once again at the thought of the school board.

"Now, class, here is you opportunity to express yourself and all that this assignment has afforded you. Yes, you have wondered for so long if you have a voice. Yes, you have felt neglected and as if you've had no purpose for societal individualism. Yes, you have something to say and want people to hear it.

"Well, here is your chance. Here is a chance for

each one of you to express yourself. This is the mark, the goal that we have been striving to reach all along. I have listened to each of you. You've talked about different areas where you believe you'll shine as the stars you are."

Emily raised her hand. "Mr. Waters, if we get up in front of the board, forgive me if I'm wrong for saying this, but if we stand before this board and give it our all and it's still not good enough then…"

"Then we can rest in the fact that you gave your best," I interrupted. "All we can do is try. All that you can do is give your best. That's why I have persisted and pushed you to give this assignment your all like your life depends on it."

I looked out over the room. The expression of sadness was plastered on the faces of my students. Even greater than the failure to give their best was that of losing me as a teacher. I was putting my entire career on the line, all to back an assignment that I believed in. I saw this class as star people in whatever avenue of life that they chose. It was a matter of all or nothing.

"All right, class, you have two days to get it together. Let's go to work and finish strong."

When I left the school, I drove over to the Madison Library off of Madison Avenue. I walked inside and was greeted by the librarian at the counter.

"Good afternoon, sir, can I help you find something?" the lady behind the counter said.

I looked at her name tag. Peggy McMillan. "Yes, how are you, Peggy? I'm looking for a book. I'm not sure if you have it or not, but it's by the author, Cornell Jones, and the title of the book is *Epic View and Epic*

*You.*"

Peggy walked to the computer and ran a search. I stood there and examined the room as Peggy punched keys on the keyboard. There was several patrons who were gathering books here and there.

"Yeah, I heard it mentioned on television the other evening," I added as I walked to the shelf with her.

Peggy reached on the shelf and pulled the book from where it was placed. "There it is, sir. Did you want to check it out?"

"Yes, ma'am," I replied, walking back to the counter with her.

"Do you have a library account with us?" Peggy asked.

I reached in my book bag and pulled out a notebook where I kept all of my school paraphernalia. I looked inside one of the pockets and pulled out my library card. I had set up a library account so that I could check out books that the school may not have carried.

"Here you go," I said, handing Peggy the card.

She took it and started plunking more keys on the keypad. "I see you carry a book bag. Are you a student?"

"Teacher," I replied. "I teach Sociology at Lawrence Higgins High."

Peggy nodded as she typed. "Hmm, that's a very controversial subject."

If I was a gullible fool, then I might've taken that as an insult. But everyone is entitled to their own opinion, even Peggy McMillan.

"Well, there is a lot of diversity in that," I said.

Peggy handed me the book and I walked out on that note.

My phone buzzed as I rode along on Highway 51. It was Tracy,

"Hey, babe," I said.

"Hey, where are you?" Tracy asked.

"On my way home."

"Listen, can you stop by the school before you get there? How far are you?"

"Not that far," I replied. "Are you okay?"

There was a short pause. "Yeah, yeah I'm fine. Just run by here before you head out."

There was a distant sound that something was wrong. I made a turn and headed to Vicksburg.

# 22

I EXITED OFF Interstate 20 and was now making my way to Hawkin Heights Middle School. When I came up on the parking lot, there were a few cars still left. I parked and walked to the entrance door.

The door was still unlocked so I assumed that lockdown hadn't started yet. Walking down the hall, I saw Tracy's office door was open and there were sounds of chatter as I neared it. When I reached the room, there was Tracy and two other teachers standing in a circle talking.

"Yes, and we can just tie up any loose ends tomorrow," Tracy said, cutting the conversation short so that the teachers would leave.

The two ladies walked to the door together. One nodded and the other smiled with eyes of disdain. I would have entertained the expression, but I had more important things to concern myself in.

"Hey, honey," Tracy said, walking to her desk and gathering together papers. "How was your day?"

I bobbed my head slightly, shaking the thought

of what that teacher might've implied before she left the room.

"Fine," I replied. "Just fine. So, what's up?"

Tracy took a seat in the chair behind her desk. "Sit with me for just a minute."

I frowned, but followed suit just as she did, grabbing the chair in front of her desk and dragging it over beside her. Tracy leaned back in her chair, smiling. I returned the smile but wondered what this whole drive out here was all about. Tracy turned to me and leaned forward as she took me by my hands.

"Honey, let me ask you something," Tracy said. "This whole assignment that you're doing, all the efforts and the progression forward… don't you think it's time to consider the summary of it and bring it to a close?"

I looked puzzled. "What? Tracy, what are you talking about?"

"I'm talking about the magnitude of all of this," Tracy replied, releasing my hands. "Dev, you know I'm not saying that I'm losing faith in you, but this whole…"

"Tracy, where is all of this coming from?" I interrupted. "What, you had me drive all the way over here for this?"

Tracy stood up. I rose to my feet too, and started to pace back and forth in front of her desk.

"Devon, you know I'm simply offering you something to think about; I'm not trying to break you down."

"Where is all this coming from, huh?" I said. "Is this what you and those other two women were in here discussing?"

"No, Devon, you know that I wouldn't do that to you. All right, I was just thinking about this whole situation and all the controversies behind it."

"Why are you doing this now?" I said sharply. "Of all the times we've talked and all…"

"I know we've talked, Devon," Tracy interrupted.

The conversation was becoming heated. The only thing I hoped was that someone wouldn't come rushing down the hall and fathom the idea of two adults arguing in a school room, a husband and a wife at that.

"Tracy, look, I don't know where all of this is coming from, but I really can't do this now."

I turned and walked to the door.

"So you just gonna leave like that?" Tracy said.

I turned around swiftly and walked back to her. "Trace, baby, I love you, but I don't want to argue with you, okay. So I'm gonna…"

"I'm not trying to argue, Devon. I'm trying…"

"I don't know what you're doing," I exclaimed. "We keep with the back and forth and all, but I…"

"I lost Alyssa in our project!" Tracy cried. "You want to know the truth? Alyssa, the lady that I was working with on the project that we had for the young adult girls, well she… she is no longer working with me on this project."

I frowned, "Wait a minute, what, did something happen to her, or did she just up and quit, or…?"

"She dropped out from the project," Tracy replied. "She said this whole issue with her uncle and that celebrity assignment's controversy was just…"

My mind boggled. This whole dispute with the

assignment that I had posed to my class, and the issues that surrounded it was at my school in another town. How this spread from Madison to Vicksburg was what was puzzling me.

I wondered how Tracy would take the news about my job as a teacher being at risk, considering the weight of this new ordeal with Alyssa.

"So tell me, Tracy," I said. "How did what's happening at Lawrence Higgins end up way over here at Hawkin Heights?"

Tracy eased back down in her chair. "Well, you know that Mr. Buckley is her uncle so I'm pretty sure that it didn't take much for the word of mouth to spread."

I cupped my chin.

"Wow, I guess it don't take much then does it?" I walked over to Tracy and squatted down in front of her, taking her now by the hands. "Babe, I'm sorry to hear that, and I'm sorry if I yelled at you and all that. I know that the both of you were working so hard on this."

Tracy leaned back and stared away. I knew that I couldn't tell her about the proposition between Mr. Donnell and me, at least not at this moment.

"So what are you gonna do now?" I asked.

Tracy sighed, closing her eyes and shaking her head slowly. "We can still go on with the project. There were several other teachers involved so, losing one won't hurt us. It's just, it's just that I really hated to see Alyssa cancel out."

"Did she say why she dropped out?" I asked. "Surely she had to give some reason why."

"You just have to know Alyssa," Tracy replied.

"Alyssa's a very reserved person so she kinda keeps to herself in a lot of matters."

"Did she say anything about Mr. Buckley?"

"No, she just said that a lot was going on, and a lot on her mind. Plus, she did mention about stuff that she had heard about students doing an assignment, and an anti-celebrity rally and all of that."

Jerry Kendell, I shouldn't have been surprised. He was trying to cut a path for himself.

"Did she say how she knew about this anti-celebrity rally, or if there was one?" I asked.

"No, there was a teacher here at the school said that she did see a flyer hanging somewhere in Jackson. She lives there."

"And we do, too," I added. "Come to think of it, Jerry was talking to several neighbors about doing a rally. I mean, Jerry's acting like a jerk."

"Which is why I'm telling you to draw the line," Tracy said. "Draw it before this whole thing gets way out of hand."

I stood up. "Well, we will soon. Friday is the deadline for this assignment. We have two days left so we'll ride it out until then."

"Good," Tracy said, relieved. "Maybe we can move on from this whole ordeal."

I looked at Tracy faintly. "Trace, I gotta tell you something, babe."

I resumed my squatting position at Tracy's knees. I took her by the hands once again slowly. Tracy hinted a frown, bracing herself as if I was about to relay some bad news.

"Mr. Donnell approached me this morning in regards to that assignment that I given to the class." I sighed. "He talked about drawing the line on this assignment, but I made him a proposition."

"Proposition?" Tracy said. "Wait a minute, I don't get it. He told you to call off that assignment?"

"Yeah, but I made an agreement with him. You see, my students have put a lot into this assignment. A lot of work has been done to help establish a voice for them. That Buckley incident shook everyone up, and a lot of people were affected by it."

Tracy released my hands, leaning back in her chair and rubbing the temples of her head. "Okay, Dev, so Mr. Donnell called off the assignment and you and he made an agreement? What agreement, Devon?"

Here went the moment of truth. From the nature of our conversation, the pressure was already heightened. But I had to be honest with her and speak as one who had faith that everything would work out for the greater good in the end.

"I told Mr. Donnell to allow the class to present their papers before the school board," I said. "Friday morning in the school auditorium my class will present their papers before the school board. When the board hears the students' voice in regards to this assignment, and the weight of it, a decision will be made."

"Decision?" Tracy said.

"If the board feels that this assignment was a help to the students, and they find favor, we win. The voice for my class is established and justice can prevail. We then can spread the inspiration and voice among the student body, encouraging them to look beyond this incident and to impacting influence from student to student. This will help in the students seeing that they can be star people in whatever they choose after they graduate."

"And if the board opposes?" Tracy said.

I glanced down at the floor then back up at her.

"I'm replaced, and Mr. Donnell finds another teacher that he feels is qualified to take my place."

"What?" Tracy said, alarmed. "Devon, you put your job on the line for this assignment? Babe, are you serious?"

"Yes," I replied, resting my forearms on Tracy's knees. "Yes, Trace, I did this and you know why? Because I believe in my class. Tracy, I know that these students wanna be heard and I believe that they have what's in 'em to be heard."

Tracy buried her face in the palm of her hands, shaking her head slowly.

"Tracy, baby, listen to me," I pleaded with my wife. "Listen, babe. All I'm asking is for you to have faith in me this one time. I know what I have dealt may sound crazy, but these students need to have a voice. Jackie's report and everything about it boiled down to having a voice. In my sense, I don't care about the celebrity, what he did, and all that. My concern is about giving my class a chance to see themselves as star people."

Tracy sat there, seeing what I was saying and at the same time wishing it were some other way.

"Jackie's report," I continued, "and everything about it boiled down to having a voice. Yeah, he reported on a celebrity, but I take it as a search deep within for the star that's within him. That's what I'm trying to bring to light. That's why I go to bat like I do. There's a star in these students that isn't just found only in movies, lights, camera, or action. Whatever field, or whatever endeavor, whatever area of expertise that they decide to excel in, that is their area of stardom."

Tracy crossed both of her arms over mine. She sighed faintly, no doubt thinking to herself, what has this man done?

"You know, Devon… I know it may seem like I don't believe in what you're doing for these kids. That's not the case, it's just… it's just that I really pray that in my heart that you don't get so engulfed in this that you end up paying for it."

She did have a point. Sometimes I could become so entangled with the affairs of school that I really didn't take close thought to things that were very important.

"You are a diligent soul," Tracy said. "I see how making a difference in your world and being a hero are two things that you are passionate about. My thing is I don't want to lose us. I'm married to you, not to Lawrence Higgins High School. You're the man I go to bed with every night, not the textbook."

We both laughed. I placed both hands on Tracy's face and gave her a kiss.

"You're right, babe," I said. "You're right. You deserve all of my time, not just the school. And, I'm sorry, I'm sorry if it seems as if we've lost us. I gave and committed my life to you not Lawrence Higgins High."

Tracy placed her arms on both sides of the chair and pushed herself up. I stood up with her.

"So you have to prove yourself Friday?" Tracy said.

"Yeah," I nodded.

"Well, you've ran the trail this long… go ahead and finish strong."

I gripped her hands gently. She gathered up her things and I helped her. Tracy turned out the light and locked the door.

"You know you owe me," Tracy said as we walked down the hall.

"Of course," I replied. "You know when it's all over I got you."

"No, I'm not talking about when it's over I'm talking about today."

I stopped in the hall. I turned to Tracy.

"Today," I said frowning. "Owe you what today?"

"Dinner," Tracy replied, smiling. "And a movie."

I laughed to myself. "I think I may be able to do that."

"You better because, if you don't me and you gonna throw down."

We both laughed. I wrapped my arm around her neck as we walked out of the school.

# 23

LATER ON THAT night I sat in the great room reading through the book I checked out from the library. Tracy had already retired for the night so I came in here so that I wouldn't disturb her. *Honey, don't stay up late. You need to go to bed.* I thought about Tracy's words. I know I should have, but that book had my attention.

I really wanted to get into this book because I was fascinated by the author's paradigms on the world we live in. Many of them I could relate to my school. I believed that my first period class had what it took to voice their opinion in a wholehearted manner for the board.

Mr. Donnell might have been right in that it seemed a little absurd to "put on" like this for the school board, but I considered it necessary. We as a class progressed this far with that assignment; why not take it all the way. Tracy was kind of skeptical on the proposal I posed, but I had faith that it would all work out for the greater good.

It was after midnight when I decided to call it

quits. I had made it through the first two chapters so I would continue at it again at another time.

The next morning I stopped by a coffee shop in Madison near McAlister's Deli. I was rushing trying to get to school so I had to make this trip snappy. If Tracy knew the kind of speed and agility I was exerting she would hammer my case about how I needed to have went to bed last night instead of staying up trying to read.

I paid for my coffee and headed out the door. As I rushed out the door I ran into someone coming in, knocking their books from their hands. I almost spilled my coffee in the process of it.

"Oh, I am so sorry," I said, bending down and helping them pick up the books.

"Ah, it's quite all right," the man said.

As I stacked and handed the books to the man I froze. It was Mr. Buckley.

"Mr. Buckley, it's… it's nice to see you."

Mr. Buckley arranged the books in his arm. "Well… Mr. Waters, same here," he said, readjusting his glasses. "You off for coffee too, huh?"

I grinned. I wondered if I should've taken the liberty to further our conversation from the other day. I knew it would make me late for school, and him too, but this might be the only chance that I would be able to get him here one-on-one.

"Mr. Buckley, I know our time is brief," I said. "But, can I ask you something?"

Mr. Buckley looked out at the parking lot then back at me.

"Sure, I guess I could spare a minute or two."

*Careful, Devon,* I thought to myself. *Be very, very careful.*

"I'm pretty sure you have heard the rave about the assignment I gave to one of my classes. However, Mr. Buckley, I am curious. You see, this assignment was birthed due to an issue that happened with you and one of your students."

"Hold on, hold on, hold on," Mr. Buckley replied. "Mr. Waters that issue has nothing to do with what you're teaching your class."

"But my class was phased by it," I interjected. "And, I'm pretty sure a lot more of the students were to."

"So what do you need to ask, Mr. Waters? Because, I need to get to class."

"What did you say to Jackie to make him smash you in the face?"

Mr. Buckley snarled a grin, nodding his head and blinking his eyes repeatedly. "No, Mr. Waters, the question is what Jackie said to me before he bashed me in the face."

Mr. Buckley walked around me and opened the door to go inside the coffee shop, and yet I still didn't get an answer. Between Jackie hitting Mr. Buckley and Mr. Buckley saying whatever he said, that's where the clarity wasn't being established.

I walked to my car and then on over to the school.

"All right, let me have everyone's attention," I said, settling the class. "Okay, tomorrow morning you all are to present your papers before members of the school board."

Meagan raised her hand. "Mr. Waters, is it just gonna be us and the school board, or is the rest of the school also gonna be there?"

"As far as I know it's just you all," I replied. "At least that's what the principal and I discussed."

"Mr. W., if you fail? Are they gonna get rid of you?" Anthony asked.

I paused, thinking about how I was going to answer that. "Get rid of me, I doubt that. If anything I'll probably be moved somewhere else."

"Dang, Mr. Waters," Meagan said. "If they replace you, ain't no telling who we'll end up with."

I sat on the edge of my desk. "So, here is where you guys come into the picture. It's going to take all of you as a class to pull together and make this board believe in whatever you have written on your papers."

The class looked at me. Some of them looked at each other, also.

"So, let's go to work," I said as I walked around my desk. "Go ahead and finish up any writing you need to get done. You all need to type this assignment out. Use the proper formatting for this."

The class started shuffling their papers and preparing to work on them.

During my lunch break, I sat out on the bench outside and graded some papers from my other classes. My stomach growled slightly. I knew that I should've been eating lunch, but paperwork had the best of my time.

"Brian, you know that's not true," someone said from behind me, coming out of the front door.

It was a young man and Meagan from my first

period class. Apparently he was her boyfriend, and they were having some sort of a disagreement.

"Look, when do you have time to hang out with me?" Brian said. "Every time I turn around it's just you and all this school work crap and all."

Brian turned to walk forward, but Meagan grabbed him by his shoulder slightly, pleading with him. Brian shook Meagan's hand off of him.

"Just get at me when you have time to talk, all right?" Brian said. He turned and walked on, leaving Meagan standing there.

I put my papers back in the notebook I held. Meagan held her head down and began to cry softly. I put the notebook back in the book bag that I brought out with me, and I stood up to walk over to where Meagan was.

"Meagan, are you all right?" I asked, placing a hand on her shoulder.

She looked up at me with tear-filled eyes. "Yeah, yes sir, Mr. Waters," she replied and slumped head swiftly.

"Meagan, what's going on? What was that all about?"

Meagan wiped the tears from her eyes with both hands. "I don't know, Brian just has a funny way of acting sometimes."

"How, I mean, what was that whole scene about?"

"Well, he had mentioned about some party with a couple of friends this weekend. I told him that I wasn't gonna be able to go because I had exams to study for all weekend."

"You taking advanced courses?" I asked.

"Yes, sir," Meagan replied. "Several of my classes are college credited courses. I'll graduate at the end of this semester and I'll start my college courses for MSU."

"Mississippi State University?" I said.

"Yes, sir, that's where I plan to go. I wanna try to get into an RN program there, if I can."

I walked a step closer to Meagan, placing another hand on her shoulder.

"Meagan, I want you to listen to me. Now, I don't know the nature of your relationship with Brian, but there is one thing that I am certain of. I listened to you in class, I've reviewed and graded your assignments all down through the semester, and you have proven yourself exceptionally. Yeah, some may pass you off as some sort of a ditzy blonde."

Meagan giggled.

"But your work far outshines your looks," I continued, "and whether Brian is dating you because you're on the cheer squad, or what have you, you must definitely show that you can't judge a book by its cover."

Meagan smiled warmly.

"Thank you, Mr. Waters."

I placed my hands in my pockets.

"Meagan, I'm not telling you to feel bad about what Brian has said or done; I'm simply saying to you to not lose focus on your dream. You stated the other day in class about your mother dying of breast cancer. In your own right, you are the star that you said you were, and the person that this whole assignment is trying to bring out of you."

I gave Meagan a chance to soak that statement

up.

"Follow the dream. Follow that dream until the end. Don't do this whole assignment for me. Don't do it just because you have to present it in front of a school board. Do it for you. Meagan, most importantly, do it for your mother."

The tears started forming again in Meagan's eyes. As we stood there, Judy, the secretary, walked out from the front door.

"Is everything all right out here?" Judy said. "Meagan, are you okay?"

Meagan turned around.

"Yes, Mrs. McClaire, Mr. Waters was just helping me with something."

Judy looked at us with a hint of suspicion.

"I promise you, Mrs. McClaire, I haven't done anything wrong," I said. "If you need, Meagan, can you go with Mrs. McClaire and tell her what's going on?"

Meagan nodded and walked to Judy. Judy was trying to reason and put the pieces to the puzzle together. She looked at me, accepting what I said to be fair and true. Meagan was a good kid with a lot of potential. As a teacher to a student, I wanted to try and direct that star that I could see in her.

The bell rang, ending lunch. I picked up my book bag from the bench. I had longed for that hero person in myself and, as time progressed, more and more of that person was shining forth.

# 24

LATER THAT AFTERNOON I gathered my things together as I wrapped up my day. I thought about my first period class and how on tomorrow if they would present themselves well. On top of that, my job was on the line.

I didn't know of any other teacher at this school who would stretch the limit as far as I had. Tracy, as much as she really believed in me, even thought that I was pushing it pretty far. Maybe I was exaggerating it, but I had faith in myself and my students. I really believed that they had the ability to prove themselves before that school board. We were either going to succeed or fail.

"So, you sure you don't want to get out of this?" Mr. Donnell said, startling me as he stood in the doorjamb.

I smiled and sighed at that statement. "Yes sir, Mr. Donnell, I'm sure."

I thought that funny how he showed up on the

scene seemingly as an intrusion to my thoughts and sentiments.

Mr. Donnell walked into the room.

"Devon, you know that you don't have to do this. I don't think that it's serious enough to get the board involved. Now, we can drop this whole thing and just pretend like it didn't exist..."

"Have you told them, the board members?" I interjected. "Did you tell them how I was risking my job for the sake of this assignment?"

Mr. Donnell folded his arms, sitting on the edge of my desk.

"Yeah, I did. Yeah, Devon, I told them. They thought it pretty peculiar for a teacher to make a bargain like you, and had wanted to see the nature of this assignment. But... if that's a decision you made they could at least hear you out."

"So, what happens, Mr. Donnell? What happens if I lose in this bout?"

"Well, the finality of it all comes down to the board. Yeah, I'm the principal, and I could get rid of you or replace you, but the totality of it is going to weigh heavily on what they think."

I tapped my pen on the desk as Mr. Donnell talked. Either way, win or lose, I had confidence in what I was doing.

"Mr. Donnell, time will tell," I said, gathering my things as I stood up. I held out my hand. "May the best man win." I walked out of the door, leaving Mr. Donnell sitting on the edge of the desk.

I cranked up as I prepared to leave. As I rode to the edge of the road I saw bumper to bumper cars over on the other side of Jones and Main Street. I turned north on Jones Street out of curiosity to see what the big stir was about.

The cars were arranged and lined bumper to bumper off of Madison Parkway in a grassed area, spreading to form a semi circle. I noticed that there were a few barbeque pits scattered in different parts of the field. There was a large tented roof that housed the stage prop and the chairs aligned across the stage that veered from it.

I parked on the tail end of the car chain near a Methodist church. As I walked through the grass, I was approached by a white gentleman in a white T-shirt and shorts. He was a sort of chunky fellow who looked to be in his mid fifties, and he smiled underneath his baseball cap and tented lavender sunglasses.

"And how are you today, sir?" he said, smiling with his hand extended.

I was still dumbfounded and curious about what was going on.

"Fine," I replied, returning the hand shake. "Fine, what is this a fundraiser?"

"Oh no, it's a talent show event we do every year. We let our kids, and adults sometimes, showcase their talent."

I raised an eyebrow.

"We kinda make it a community oriented event," the man said. "And, we try to involve everyone. School just let out so we should be getting more kids and adults here pretty soon."

I looked around at all the people.

"That's nice. Hey, I know that kid," I said, pointing to the stage.

It was Nathan from my first period. The crowd

clapped as he walked to the stage.

"Excuse me just a moment," I said, walking toward the stage to find a seat.

Nathan walked to the stage with a paper in his hand.

"Hello, everyone. My name is Nathan, and I'm gonna read from something that was given to me. It actually comes from an assignment in one of my classes. I was asked by the teacher to answer the question of who I am. If you were to ask me that same question, I would tell you this."

I sat on the edge of my seat in anticipation. Nathan adjusted his paper as he prepared himself to read. The crowd also sat in expectancy as well.

"Who am I?" Nathan started. "I'll tell you, I am an artist with the untapped capability to sketch on the pages and even into the hearts of those I encounter, the beauty of art. I am the one whose artistic work receives notoriety from public figures miles around. I am the artist whose work will receive the attention as it is displayed and broadcast in art galleries of legends such as Thomas Kinkade.

"Some look and consider my speech as fanciful and wishful thinking. I look and consider my speech as epic as I rise portrait by portrait to the top, and am considered by those of high prestige and clout as a designer of masterpieces projected here, there, and everywhere in the world."

Everyone cheered, including me. Nathan walked to the edge of the stage as someone handed him a canvas that displayed a drawing. Nathan turned it toward the crowd.

"This here is one of my pieces of art that I

composed," Nathan said.

It was the etching of a man standing on a hill observing a valley nearby. The sky was clouded in smoke as light and rays of energy poured into the valley. The concoction from the sky beamed down, showing hues of tangerine smoke surrounding a yellow shock of energy. I for one was amazed at Nathan's artistic work.

Nathan walked off the stage and I stood up, nearing him to celebrate his work. I approached him as he was talking things over with a woman who could pass for his mother.

"Nathan," I chanted. "That was excellent."

"Mr. Waters," Nathan replied, puzzled. "What are you doing here?"

"Well, by chance I guess. I was leaving the school, but noticed all of this here going on so I stopped by. And, boy am I glad I did."

Nathan grinned sheepishly. "Yeah, I was doing it for extra credit for my art class. I have to go over here to the help table and get my sheet to take to class tomorrow."

I placed a hand on Nathan's shoulder. "Nathan, son, I'm proud of you. To come here and share from an assignment in front of a crowd of people, that's… good."

Nathan shrugged.

"And as a teacher seeing a student that makes me feel good also. To see you doing this makes me feel that what I'm doing is making a difference. I go home to my wife night after night and wonder if what I'm teaching is making y'all better people, in spite of the outside opposition."

"Mr. Waters, it's cool," Nathan said. "I think the class stuff is fine, and as far as life… everyone'll just figure it out on their own."

"But, you see, Nathan," I replied. "That's just it. My job, well it feels like my job, is to try to steer you along in the right course. Yeah, life happens to us all, but a direction in the path we choose and decisions we make… that can be aided."

"Nathan!" a woman called out, standing afar off from us. She beckoned for him to come to her.

"Oh, that's my mom. I gotta go by this table and get my sheet and head on."

I nodded. "Okay, well I'll see you in the morning. Be ready."

Nathan nodded and walked to his mother. I stood there with my hands in my pockets, reflecting on our conversation.

My phone buzzed as I rode down Highway 51, entering into Ridgeland. It was Tracy.

"Hello?"

"Hey, babe, where are you?" Tracy said on the other end of the line.

"Riding," I replied. "I'm in Ridgeland."

"Okay, well, are you on your way to the house?"

"Yeah, that's where I was heading to. What's up?"

"I need you to do me a favor when you get home," Tracy said. "You'll look in the bedroom and there should be a flyer lying on the bed. On the flyer is a telephone number scribbled on it. I need you to text me that number, please? I'll love you forever if you do."

I twisted my lips. "Love you forever? Really,

babe?"

Tracy chuckled. "You know I love you. But, for real, honey, I need that number to give to another one of the teachers. I thought I had put that piece of paper with my stuff this morning, but I guess I didn't."

"All right," I replied. "Are you gonna be late getting home?"

"I shouldn't be too late. Of course, it may be after five when I get there."

Five was late enough in my book. Maybe one of these days our lives would straighten out and we could be two people who arrived home at a reasonable time together. Maybe.

"All right, I'll send the number to you," I said.

"Muah," Tracy replied, implying the sound of a kiss. "I'll see you when I get home."

We hung up as I neared the house. I parked the car and walked in. When I was inside I laid my book bag on the counter. The coffee pot was left on, and a sheet of paper sat beside it.

"No, Tracy," I said, picking up the paper. It was a flyer with a number written at the very bottom. "No, dear, I think you left the paper here by the coffee pot."

I went into the bedroom just to verify that the paper that I was holding was the right one. After that I went and sat on the porch.

As I sat there I thought about the day I had, and the one I would have tomorrow. I thought about how this would be a turning point in my career as a teacher. I had taught at Lawrence Higgins High School for six years now. I've had the chance to teach all kinds of students. When you deal with the world from a sociological point of view it can stir up all different kinds of perspectives, and the students that I have taught proved that out.

Mr. Harrison, a man who lived down the street from me, was out walking his dog. He walked along the sidewalk with his border collie attached to the leash. Mr. Harrison was a man who looked to be in his late sixties, or early seventies.

"How are you, Mr. Harrison?" I said, waving from the porch.

Mr. Harrison stopped in mid stride.

"How you doin'?" he replied in a southern Italian accent, waving.

He turned and walked towards the house. As he did, his collie started sniffing the grass and territory she treaded frantically. I stood up and shook Mr. Harrison's hand as he approached me.

"You out for a walk huh?" I said.

"Yeah, me and Bessie decided to go for a walk. I hardly get ou' with her so, you know, gotta do it when I can."

"Well, you can have a seat if you'd like," I said, motioning to the chair beside me.

He took a seat, and Bessie sat on her hind legs beside him.

"So, did you get a chance to go to that rally the other day with Jerry Kendell?" I asked, striking up a conversation. Really it was more so to pry for information. I knew that if anyone knew about what was going on, Mr. Harrison did.

"Nah," Mr. Harrison replied in a raspy tone, waving off the question with his hand. "I ain't into all the politics, you know."

"What was that rally all about?"

"Power," Mr. Harrison exclaimed. "Influence, I tell ya, when you deal with Jerry Kendell you deal with politics."

Mr. Harrison spoke strongly in a deep Italian inflection that made him sound like a mob boss who was used to crooks and cronies trying to get over on him.

"Yeah, I've noticed that a lot of people in this town have a lot of respect for him. I mean, he must be something to have that much impact."

"Pioneer, or so he think he is," Mr. Harrison rebutted. "I had a chance to talk with him some time back."

I turned my chair in Mr. Harrison's direction. "So, who is he? I know he works down in Brookhaven, but there must be more to him than that."

"I'ma put it to you like dis," Mr. Harrison said. "Jerry Kendell is just a would-be teacher who pursued a degree years ago in the social culture arena. Problem is he never finished. He one of those guys who kinda got a inferior background, you know what I mean? He vent off his dispositions of it in an indirect manner."

"Social culture?" I said, pondering that thought.

"Yeah, I mean don't get me wrong. Jerry's a good guy, a really good guy, but his approach to things is a little distorted, you know. Jerry's kinda like an activist for the community. Whenever he feels the community is in danger, he freaks out."

I raised my eyebrows at that statement. That explained a lot.

"Yeah, he's flippin' out about some charade that happened at school and all…"

"A teacher was hit by a student," I interrupted.

"Yeah, he all in cahoots about it, and wagin' a war about it. So serious."

"I teach at a school in Madison, it's about twenty miles or so from here. A student hit a teacher, and the press behind that was because the kid did a paper for class on a celebrity who did a charity fund event up in Canton. The problem is, or the mystery rather is, what did the teacher say to make the student hit him? That's what's not being told here.

"Well I look at it like dis," Mr. Harrison said. "If the kid did wrong, discipline him and be done. Don't go around and make a big parade about it."

My phone buzzed on the little table that sat between us. It was Tracy.

"Excuse me, Mr. Harrison," I said. "Hello?"

"Hey, I'm leaving the school now," Tracy said. "And I'll be home in a little bit."

"Okay, I'm sitting on the front porch talking with Mr. Harrison from down the street."

As I talked, Bessie started barking and trying to run off the porch. Mr. Harrison tried to calm her down as she barked at another dog running down the street.

"Okay, honey, I'll talk to you when you get here."

Mr. Harrison stood there, holding Bessie by the leash. I hung up the phone with Tracy.

"Well, Mr. Harrison, I don't wanna keep you or Bessie any longer," I said, shaking his hand.

"Yeah, she geta kinda fidgety you know," Mr. Harrison said. "Look here, don't let Jerry get chu down. You keep doin' you an' ita all pay off."

Mr. Harrison walked down the steps.

"Thank you, Mr. Harrison," I said, waving Mr.

Harrison off.

A would-be teacher of social culture who never finished his degree. All of the pieces of the puzzle were starting to come together, and tomorrow my last piece of my puzzle would come together too.

# 25

"HEY, YOU UP EARLY," Tracy said groggily.

It was the next morning and I had started my day earlier than usual. I was dressing for school as I buttoned the sleeves of my shirt. I was trying a more professional approach today. Any other day I looked the part of a casual teacher, but not today.

"You're wearing a suit?" Tracy said, sitting up in the bed.

I was wearing a navy blue double vented suit and a white button down shirt.

"Yeah," I replied, adjusting my crimson colored tie in front of the dresser mirror. "Gotta look the part don't I?"

I walked over to the edge of the bed and sat down near Tracy.

"Yeah," I sighed. "The moment of truth is here."

"Where's everything gonna be at? In your

classroom?

"No, in the auditorium. We're supposed to meet in there and allow the class to express themselves."

Tracy leaned toward me. "So, who all from the school board is gonna be there?"

"I don't know," I replied. "I'm not sure if it's everybody or just a few." I placed my hand on Tracy's shoulder. "Baby, as ready for this as I am, I'm kinda nervous too at the same time."

Tracy sat back, placing a hand on the side of my face. "Dev, you've prepared yourself day in and day out for this. I'll admit, I thought it was sort of crazy to put your job on the line for this at first. But, I got to thinking about how you are so loyal and dedicated to seeing that these students shine as the stars that they are."

I smiled.

"You believed," Tracy continued, "even when I thought that the whole thing should've been dropped. You saw when I couldn't even see. Devon Waters, this is your time and your moment." Tracy cupped the sides of my face. "Do it for those kids, do it for me, your wife, but most importantly… do it for yourself."

Every fiber of Tracy's words savored into my being. I had labored day after day since I had issued that assignment, all to prove a point. To prove that the matter was bigger than Jackie, Mr. Buckley, or some essay on a celebrity.

This whole course of events was to move away from a celebrity, and to show my first period class that whatever they aspired to become after they graduated had the potential to make them stars.

I stood up, as did Tracy also, pulling the covers back. I pulled my wife to me and hugged her tight.

"I love you so, so very much," I said. "Thank you. Thank you for having my back no matter how crazy what I did may have sounded. I so promise that I'm going to make it up to you."

Tracy refrained back slightly and looked at me. "Well, we can talk about payback after it's over," Tracy teased. "But for now, go get 'em tiger," she said, winking.

I kissed her and then grabbed my coat and briefcase. I walked out to my car thinking that this day was the determining factor of my future as a teacher, or someone's presence that would become that of a distant memory.

*****

I pulled into the parking lot of Lawrence Higgins High School. I sat there in the car, thinking of how this was a no turning back moment. I stepped out of the car and grabbed my briefcase. Greg was walking by.

"Well, look at you," Greg said. "What's the occasion?"

I shut the car door. "A meeting," I replied. "That's all. Excuse me." I started walking toward the building.

Greg started yapping.

"A meeting," he said, walking along with me. "What kind of a meeting? For teachers?"

I stopped in my tracks, turning to Greg. "No, Greg, a meeting with the principal and others. Look, I really don't have time for this."

"Is this about the whole situation with Mr. Buckley? Devon, why don't you just let that whole deal go."

I felt anger starting to creep up on me. "Look, Greg, I'd love to stand here and play back and forth with you, but I have more important things to do. So, why don't you do both of us a favor and just drop it for now, and let's go on about our day?"

Greg grinned. I knew his conversation was just a taunt to throw me off track. I didn't have time for this, especially right before I was about to walk into a meeting. I left Greg standing there and walked on to the inside of the school.

I stopped by the office to look for Mr. Donnell.

"Morning, Judy, have you seen Mr. Donnell?" I asked.

Judy looked up from what she was doing. "Good morning, he was just in here a minute ago. Did you need him for something?"

"Yeah, I have a meeting this morning," I replied. "I need to talk to him."

Judy examined me and the suit I was wearing. I imagined that she was just as shocked as Greg was when he first saw me.

"I'll call him up here," Judy said, still stunned by my attire.

She summoned for Mr. Donnell over the intercom.

"Must be an important meeting," Judy said. "You're all dressed up."

I rested my briefcase on the counter above Judy's desk, leaning my arms on the counter as well.

"Well, it is," I said. "Meeting with the school board this morning."

Mr. Donnell came walking into the office as I spoke. "Devon," he said surprised. "Now aren't you all suited up and ready for this morning?"

I cut a slight grin. "As I told my wife before I came, gotta look the part."

Mr. Donnell chuckled. "What can I do for you?"

"I was just checking with you about the meeting with the board, and trying to see where we all needed to be."

"Oh yes," Mr. Donnell said, looking at his watch. "I talked to Donnie Reagan, who's a member of the board, and he said that he'd be here for eight-thirty."

"So, we're meeting in the auditorium?" I asked.

"Yes," Mr. Donnell replied. "You and your class could meet us in there. Did you mention to them about wardrobe?"

"I told them about the meeting with the board, and I mentioned to them about presentation and making themselves presentable for this day."

Mr. Donnell nodded. There was still that hint of suspense about my decision to meet before the school board members. At this point I was clear on my intent. I had progressed this far so there was no point in going back now.

"Okay, Devon, well I also talked to Mr. Buckley and asked if he could attend this meeting as well."

"Really?" I replied. "Well, that'll make our time spent all the more better."

Mr. Donnell stepped in closer to me. "Devon, I

really hope that you know what you're doing here."

I raised an eyebrow. "Mr. Donnell, I am sure on my part. It ain't time to be scared now, so let's just trust that everyone does their part."

The bell rang, breaking our conversation. I went and grabbed my briefcase from the counter and walked down the hall to my classroom.

"Well, I hope you're all ready," I said to the class, sitting on the edge of my desk.

We were moments away from our meeting with members of the school board.

"Mr. Waters," Emily said, raising her hand. "I just want to say that no matter what the board decides, you are still my teacher."

"Thank you, Emily. And you all are still my students. It is my hopes that you all have put the critical thinking needed to hopefully let your voices be heard."

"Hey, Mr. Waters," Anthony called out. "You think if we do good, then the school board can kinda cut Jackie some slack?"

"I don't know, Anthony," I replied. "All we can do is hope for the best."

A knock came at the door. It was Mr. Donnell.

"Hey, Dev, are you ready? The board is on their way over here."

"Yes sir, Mr. Donnell," I replied. "Just getting the class ready."

"Okay, well it's ten till," Mr. Donnell said. "I'm about to head on down to the auditorium."

Mr. Donnell closed the door. I instructed everyone to gather their reports and we walked on down to the auditorium.

# 26

THE CLASS AND I sat together on the first row of seats in the auditorium. I could tell the nervousness that the class was feeling. I myself was sort of anxious, too.

"Well, hello, Mr. Reagan," Mr. Donnell said in the distance behind me, standing at the entrance door.

I turned in my seat as Mr. Reagan and three other members of the school board walked in behind him. I stood up and walked back to where they were.

"Hello, Mr. Reagan," I said, extending my hand out.

Mr. Reagan shook my hand. "Hi, Mr. Waters, I brought with me some of the other members." Mr. Reagan turned and held out his arm to present the other members. "This is Susan McCorrmick, Scott Winfred, and Paula Juniper."

I smiled and shook everyone's hand. Judging by the smiles and personality vibe in the air, everyone seemed to be modest. Of course, looks could be deceiving too.

Donnie Reagan was a tall, slender man with rectangular glasses. His bespectacled, narrow face reminded me of a computer genius who built a piece of software that revolutionized the world.

Susan McCorrmick, on the other hand, was a short, chirpy faced woman with crystal blue eyes and too much makeup. Her coal black hairdo was overdone, and added the image of excess narcissism. Scott Winfred was a balding, middle-aged man who could pass for a college dropout who invented some bizarre idea that baited its followers in by its spectacle of grandeur.

Then, you had Paula Juniper. She was a small woman with short brown hair highlighted with blonde streaks. She grimaced at nothing in particular, but gave the notion of one who wouldn't have a problem sharing a piece of her mind if need be, or if she was given the opportunity.

"It's a pleasure to meet you, Devon," Susan said, smiling. "Are these all here your students?"

I turned around to face my class sitting on the front row. "Yes, this is my first period class. Some bright students," I bragged.

"Yeah, I understand that you all did an assignment?" Scott said.

"Yes sir. Well, it was actually an assignment that flowed into one of our subjects." I clasped my hands together. "An incident occurred a couple of weeks ago, I'm pretty sure you've heard about it, and it sort of disturbed the class."

"Disturbed?" Donnie said. "What do you mean by that?"

"The whole drama about the student's arrest," I

replied. "You know, everyone wondered what caused it. What caused the student to tick and hit the teacher in the face?"

Concern beamed from everyone's face.

"I kinda wondered what was said too," I added.

"And that's why we're here," Mr. Donnell said, placing his hands behind his back swiftly. "Uh, Mr. Reagan, Devon and I talked about this assignment, and he thought it would be good to allow the class to read their essays before you to leave the final decision up to you."

All the members of the board looked at each other and nodded their heads.

"Very well then," Donnie said. "Let's see what you have."

We all walked toward the front where the students were, and the stage. The class passively turned their heads in our direction. I looked at them and grinned. This was the moment of truth.

As we all stood there and prepared to get into our presentations, Mr. Buckley came walking through the entrance door.

"You can come on down too, Mr. Buckley," Mr. Donnell said, beckoning with his hand. Mr. Buckley came striding slowly down the aisle with a manila folder in his hand.

While Mr. Donnell, Mr. Buckley, and the board spoke briefly among themselves, I walked over to my students. I stood there in front of them and encouraged them like a football coach cheering the team to take the win.

"All right, Devon, we're ready," Mr. Donnell said.

The class sat in the front of the right section of the auditorium. The principal, teacher, and the school board members sat in the center section on the front row. The lights were dimmed in the auditorium, and the stage lights beamed the stage.

I walked onto the stage to present our class and the assignment.

"Well, good morning everyone," I said, standing near the edge of the stage. "Teachers and school board members, I am glad that you all are here this morning for this occasion."

Mr. Donnell grinned as he whispered something to Donnie who sat left of him.

"I would like to thank Mr. Donnell for giving us the chance to do this, and also I want to say thank you to the board members for taking the time out of your schedules to partake also in this special occasion."

It was my desire that Mr. Buckley would see the impact and importance of this assignment, and the message that I was trying to get over to him and to others.

"I know we're time sensitive," I said. "So, why don't we get right to it? This assignment was birthed because a dilemma was created that caused frustration and anguish among my first period class. A student from another class retaliated to a response that one of our teachers, Mr. Buckley, made. I, or we rather, don't have the time to delve into that now."

Mr. Buckley sat there with a grimacing look plastered on his face. I wasn't at this point trying to make an attack, but was hoping that the board would see the whole of this in moderation.

"I'm going to ask Emily, Meagan, Nathan, and

Anthony to come and join me on stage."

The four students all arose simultaneously. Anthony was stunned, but stood up and followed suit with the others. The rest of the class sat there appeased, relieving within that they weren't summoned to come stand with me in utter nervousness.

The four students stood alongside me. "Board members, these are the select group of my choosing who I would like to open up this presentation. The rest of the class will follow suit, if time permits, and from there the decision will be turned over to you."

The school board members nodded. I stepped back, as did the four chosen students. I made a motion to Emily to start the presentation. Emily bowed her head and stepped forward with her paper in her hand.

"Good morning," Emily said. "The title of this essay is The I Am Assignment. When Mr. Waters first asked us to do this, I was somewhat nonchalant about it and even thought that this assignment held zero weight."

I grinned at that statement.

"But as the days passed," Emily continued, "I began to see facets of my life unfold and am very grateful to Mr. Waters for this assignment."

Emily held up her paper and began reading.

The I Am Assignment, an assignment given in light of a dilemma among a fellow student. This assignment was given to demystify the glamour of lights, camera, and action on some red carpet. It was given to show that we are stars as well in any field that we can master and successfully shine. My area of I AM:

**Emily, the Life Coach**

**There are so many battered women hurting in a warped society that is filled with delusion, hurt, broken trust, and lust-mistaken love. I Am one that sees so many of these women in my world and society who falls prey to the downfalls and sound-good speeches from the guy who has nothing more than a fast tongue to offer to a feeble-minded woman. I Am one who fell prey to a soothsaying speech and lost the pureness of who I was to someone who abused my kindness and trust. I Am one who has sat alone in the darkest of hours crying on the bathroom floor with only the thought of how my life was a wreck. Nevertheless, I Am one whose purpose is to coach other battered women in life and to help these women not follow down the same path that I did. And with that, that's why I Am Emily, the Life Coach.**

Emily paused, fighting back the tears of her presentation. The class of students, and the school staff, clapped behind Emily's presentation. Emily walked over to me and gave me a hug, and then exited the stage to return to her seat. I stood there trying to pull myself together.

For a school assignment to be taken serious, Emily punctuated that. It baffled me how this was a student who exemplified the critical thinking measure of this assignment.

Nathan stepped forward next to read his paper. "Good morning, I would like to present to you my definition of The I Am Assignment." Nathan raised his paper to read.

## I Am Nathan, the Artist

**When I was asked to present this paper to Mr. Waters to turn in for a grade, I thought that this assignment was kind of ridiculous. I even questioned whether or not this essay would make an impact or just be some paper to fill in time for class. But as I progressed with it, I began to see the weight of it unfold. I was given an opportunity to present my artwork before a large group, even Mr. Waters stopped by to see my work. It was then that I could say if stardom and celebrity had a name, then I would classify it as the artist. Yes, I Am the Artist who exemplifies the art of creative expression. I Am Nathan, the Artist, who has sketched my stage and masterpiece of stardom through artistic expression. I do etch and paint the picture of my own world of art. Celebrity, glamour, and glitz have pinnacled our society, whether by mirages or facades that baits a binge on the people involved with it. Well, I know if time and chance are given, then I would pave my own path by pouring from the sketches to the pad a picture of surrealism that flows from the heart of Nathan, the Artist.**

Everyone clapped once again as Nathan shook my hand and walked off the stage. The school board members talked amongst themselves softly as we prepared for the next presentation. Mr. Donnell and Mr. Buckley chattered a few words as they sat there.

I thought to myself on how these students were giving one hundred percent more than I expected. The final decision would be made from the school board members, but I believed that we had enough momentum for them to give some serious thought to it.

# 27

AS EVERYONE SETTLED themselves and prepared for the next presenters, I stood there in anticipation and excitement. I could feel the energy and the suspicion of thoughts that flooded the board members' minds. This was a very critical time for my students. Not just for them, but for me as well.

Anthony was next to present his essay. He hesitated before stepping forward. I could see the nervousness and apprehension on his face, thinking to himself if he could do this. In a no-turning-back motion, Anthony stepped forward to the center stage.

"Uh, my name is Anthony," he said, flustered. "And, today my I Am assignment is about…" Anthony paused as he stood there examining the audience. "My I Am assignment…" Anthony sighed as if he were speechless. I stood on the side, encouraging him that he could do this.

Anthony looked over at me then out at the audience. He dropped his head briefly, trying to build up confidence to say what he had to say.

"You know, if there is anyone who thought this assignment was lame it was me," Anthony said. "I remember all of those times in class when Mr. Waters kept pushing us about this paper, and all I could think of was how this was a big waste of time. Some moments it was like are we in class or is he some kinda psychologist?"

Everyone laughed softly.

"But," Anthony continued, "now I see the importance of this assignment. I remember Mr. Waters asked me if I had started on the assignment. I told him I did, but was hesitant in my speech… until today. If I had to give an I Am for this assignment, then it would read like this."

**I Am Anthony, the Parole Officer**

**I grew up and live in a place where dudes of all sorts thrive off of the high and vibe of a good time. What's a good time? Maybe steal a little, get a little. Maybe to smoke a little or slang a little for that money that comes fast that it's easy. I watched my big brother ride in and out of jail so many times it worried my mother sick. I watched my mother work her fingers to the bone just to make ends meet for us. So you ask why I want to be a parole officer? I say it's because I've seen enough dudes in my lifetime to keep the prisons hot, and if I can do anything about it I will. This is not a say no to drugs, get crime off the street speech. This is Anthony saying if I could make a mark, or build some kind of stage for stardom in my book, odd as that sounds, it would be me going down in history for being one who did his part so that someone else could spare the drama.**

**Yeah, spare the drama and play their parts on this grand stage of life, as Mr. Waters would say. I'm sorry if this paper is grammatically incorrect, but just know that it's from me speaking my piece as Anthony, the Parole Officer.**

The atmosphere froze. In all the time that I had Anthony as a student, never once had I heard him speak with such zeal and realism until this moment. Anthony walked off the stage. As he did, the handclaps built into an uproar of cheer. I walked swiftly to stop Anthony before he walked to sit down. I hugged him tightly. I knew beneath that façade of a front there was a kid inside who was built to do something great.

Anthony went and took his seat. The board members continued to talk in a seated huddle. The class sat with great prediction, awaiting the final outcome of this all.

"Well, I hope you all have enjoyed the essays and presentations thus far," I said, standing center stage. "We are down to the last of the four, and following that I'll turn it over to you all for the further of our morning presentations."

I stepped back as Meagan walked to the center of the stage. "Hello, my name is Meagan, and here is my presentation of the I Am assignment."

**I Am Meagan, the Registered Nurse**

**In light of this I Am Assignment, odd as it may have seemed in the beginning, it wasn't until later on as the days went by that I could stand in perfect harmony and give you my perfect definition of I Am.**

**I Am one who stood and watched her mother lose her**

**life two years ago at the hands of breast cancer. I Am also one who watched this same woman give it her all just so that I could have it all. It was then that I harbored the pain inside of losing my best friend in the entire world, and someone that knew me inside and out. But I am thankful to Mr. Waters for allowing me this chance to search inside where greatness lies in order to finally, after all this time, be able to give perfect definition to the caliber of person that resides inside me. So you ask who I Am? I'll tell you. I Am the Registered Nurse who has taken it upon herself in the wake of calamity to help save as many lives, especially of cancer patients, as I can. In honor of my friend, my jewel, and my heart, my mother, I will do what I have to do to make sure I can prevent and protect the lives of those who live in infirmity. Yes, I'll do this all as Meagan, the Registered Nurse. That is who I Am.**

Everyone stared, baffled. I walked over to Meagan slowly. The tears were falling from her face after giving a very heartfelt presentation. The outcome and reality of this assignment had turned out greater than I expected.

I placed a hand on Meagan's shoulder.

"You okay?"

She nodded her head. I turned and looked down at the school board members as they sat and wrapped up their remaining notes from the presentation.

"Ladies and gentlemen," I said. "The readings and presentations given this morning were beyond what I expected. You've heard different perspectives of what a star is and what their stage of stardom looks like. You definitely can't judge a book by its cover. In my case, Anthony proved that for me."

I looked at Anthony as he sat there calm, cool, and collected. I glanced at my watch.

"I know that we are all pressed for time, so if it's all right with you I'll let it rest at the four and you can take the remaining students' papers with you to base your decision on the class as a whole."

The members of the board nodded their heads as they looked at one another.

"This assignment was given to everyone as a result of an occurrence between a teacher and another student," I said, looking at Mr. Buckley.

Mr. Buckley looked at me firmly as he exhaled a sigh.

"The student retaliated," I continued, "to that teacher's remarks and comments and was arrested for his actions. My class was in an uproar behind it, so I presented them with an assignment. This assignment flowed right along with a chapter of our study from the textbook.

"As distorted as this project may seem to you, my intentions were not to justify that student's actions. The student did a report over a celebrity, responded to the teacher's remark with a jab, and was arrested. Now, it's the 'what' of those remarks that has yet to be disclosed…"

"That's not the point," Mr. Buckley interrupted. "That's not the way to reply or handle things."

"As I've said, board members," I said, ignoring Mr. Buckley's comment. "My intention with this essay assignment was to redirect my class's attention away from the celebrity glamour and glitz out in the world, and allow them to find the star in them."

I walked over to the side of the stage in front of my class. "You've heard four accounts of what several of the students desire to do after graduation. Why not build a platform of stardom from that?"

Donnie stood up with his notebook in his hand.

"All right, here's what we're going to do. First of all, excellent job on the presentations this morning," he said, facing in the class's direction. He turned and looked at me. "Devon, we would like to take those papers and review them over. Monday we will have made an executive decision on how we're going to handle the direction of all these events overall. As for now, this meeting's adjourned and everyone can go on to their classes and carry on about their day."

The students stood up and I walked down from the stage and collected their papers to give to the board. As I walked to where they were I saw Mr. Donnell and Mr. Buckley chattering about something. I handed the papers to Donnie.

"Thank you, Mr. Reagan, for you and the board taking time out of your schedules for this," I said to him as I handed him the papers.

"That was real good," Susan said, nodding along with the rest of the board members.

I bid my farewell and escorted my class back to the room.

"Mr. Buckley, I'd like to have a word with you in Mr. Donnell's office," Donnie said, as the class and I exited the auditorium.

I in no way desired to pose as a villain in this matter. My intentions were clear, and from the students' presentation I believed my point to be made. Now it

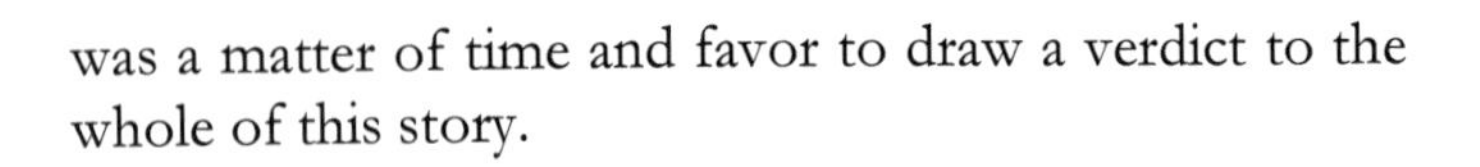


was a matter of time and favor to draw a verdict to the whole of this story.

# 28

"SO, WHAT DID you think?" I said, sitting on my desk.

The class and I were back in the room and rehearsing the presentations that were given. I felt so proud of my class. Even though the entire room didn't present their papers, the weight of the ones that did held for the entire class.

Emily raised her hand. "Mr. Waters, I would like to say something on behalf of the whole class." She stood up beside her desk. "I think I can speak on behalf of the class when I say that I think that everyone here, whether you read your paper or not, represented this class well."

I bowed my head to that.

"For us who read, that was kinda deep, Mr. Waters," Emily continued, "and for us to reach inside and share stuff that we wouldn't dare reveal in an everyday conversation, that really says a lot."

"Which is why they gotta give us our props," Anthony interrupted. "I mean, Mr. W., you know me and where I stand. All class long you kept tryin' to get me to read this and read that, but it wasn't 'til I thought about how they was jockin' you and ya job. It's like, why is e'rybody takin' what you doin' so serious?"

I bobbed my head to that. This assignment had put us all under pressure, me in particular. I hopped off of the desk.

"First of all," I said. "I want to say that I am so, so, so proud of every one of you. I truly believe if time allotted, and everybody had the chance to read their papers, I know that everyone would have given it their all one hundred percent.

Nathan raised his hand. "Mr. Waters, where do we go from here?"

"Well, Nathan," I said, starting my pace back and forth in front of my desk. "Monday is the big day that will determine whether we can continue on in our class, or if I will be replaced with someone else."

"Mr. Waters, they can't just get rid of you," Meagan said. "You have helped to change everyone's perspective in this class. When we started out, everybody thought that this was just another philosophy class or something. But you changed the game for all of us. You helped us to look inside and find the star in all of us, beyond the TV screen and red carpet."

Meagan arose from her desk and walked toward me.

"Mr. Waters, if anyone can show that there is a star person in you," she said, placing her hand on my arm. "It would have to be you."

I glanced down, nodding my head. After all the sessions we had in class, after all the days of wondering if what I was saying was making a difference, it was this moment here that made me feel that my assignment to this class was accomplished.

"Thank you, Meagan," I said. I walked around behind my desk and took a seat. "And thank all of you. It has been a pleasure in teaching you thus far, and it has been an honor to me for you to take this assignment to heart."

The class all looked around at each other, reflecting on the warmth of inspiration that filled the room.

"Let's just wait until Monday," I said. "And let's finish strong."

I sat on my couch that evening reflecting on the morning that I had. I was so proud of my class, and I was especially proud of the read of presentations. Emily, Nathan, Anthony, and Meagan went far beyond what I expected. Those weren't just essay papers, but heartfelt inspirations of the dreams that were harbored in their hearts. Potential yet to be tapped but not yet disclosed.

Tracy was late getting home. I got up off the couch and walked to the refrigerator to get a snack. As I walked to it a knock came at the door. I walked to the front door, tired from the long day's work that I had put in.

I opened the front door. I would almost be inclined that this was a dream, but I knew it wasn't.

"Devon Waters," Jerry Kendell said, standing there holding a rolled up newspaper and a smile on his face.

"Can I help you with something?" I said.

"Oh no," he replied. "I was just coming over to congratulate you on your little presentation this morning."

I wondered where he heard that. It fascinated me how news from Madison made it to Jackson. Jerry's speech hinted sarcasm. He wasn't here to applaud my efforts no more than I was going to applaud his.

"What do you want, Jerry?"

"I heard that some students from your class did some presentations and I…"

"Had to come over here and throw my little two cents in your face," I said, finishing his humor.

Jerry looked at me wryly.

"Look, Jerry, if you're coming over here to try and bust my bubble with some lame speech about what you're doing, save it. All right, I done took about all I can from you."

"You need to be aware of something," Jerry replied. "You're not the only one who can get on a sociological level with this. You wanna do culture and trend talk…"

"Let me ask you something?" I interrupted. "If you're so cultured in this sociological move, why didn't you finish your degree for it?"

Jerry rolled his neck at me. "Excuse me?"

"If you're such a big shot in being an activist for the community, and trying to set everyone in their place, why not finish the degree and go into a field where you would be that effective scholar in the cultural analysis?"

Jerry under eyed me, snarling a grin.

"Yeah, I know," I said. "A would-be teacher of social culture, but he dropped out and went in another direction."

"Boy, you better…" Jerry replied, furious.

"You came on my property," I said fervently. "You wanna take it to the head, then let's go. You go around doing rallies and front porch speeches about how we need to clean up the community, but really you're taking shots at me. You're shooting me down before you can get a clear understanding of what I'm doing. I'm not up in class trying to promote celebrities and Hollywood and all that. I'm taking a group of students and showing them that they have every much of a right to get superb recognition in their pursuits after they all graduate. Being a celebrity doesn't make you a star; the ability to master and bring value to this world – that's what makes somebody a star."

Jerry stood there, dumbfounded by my words. It didn't matter to me if I had to go to the extremes with him. At this phase of the mission it was no time to turn around and go back.

Jerry nodded his head. "Okay, all right… if that's your take on this, fine. We'll see the verdict of this whole matter. And, if you're so stuck on your point, that's fine. Yeah, that's fine, because you can rest assure that I am definite on mine."

He walked off the porch and to his truck. As he was getting in the truck, Tracy was turning in the driveway. Jerry cranked up and rode along from the curb. I walked out to meet Tracy under the carport.

"Hey, what did he want?" Tracy said, grabbing shopping bags from the passenger seat and stepping out of the car.

"Keeping tabs," I replied. "Where have you been? What's this, we going shopping now?"

Tracy looked at the bags as she raised them. "No, I just ran by the mall to pick up a couple of things."

I stared, appalled.

"What?" Tracy said grinning. "Can't a sister go to the mall?"

I still held the same visage. "I'm thinking you're still at the school and you're out on a shopping spree."

Tracy wrapped her arms around my neck. "I sorry, baby. You know I love you."

I tried to hold a serious countenance, but the humor of Tracy dampened the moment. All I could do was cackle at her. She shuttered my talk with constant kisses between words.

"It's all love, babe," Tracy said, hugging me tight. "Hmm, I love you."

I held my arms around Tracy with my head lying on her shoulder. "I love you too."

We let each other go as Tracy shuffled her bags in her hand. "You'll grab my briefcase, babe out of the backseat for me?"

I walked to her car as she walked inside the house. I grabbed her briefcase and shut the door, looking out at the neighborhood and recollecting on my conversation with Jerry.

"So what was that all about on the front porch earlier?" Tracy said.

We were now eating dinner at the table. Tracy whipped up a quick meal. We were having lemon chicken sandwiches with arugula and pears and chips on the side.

I held up my sandwich as I prepared to take a

bite.

"Jerry wanted to infiltrate a congratulations to me," I replied, taking a bit of the sandwich and talking with a full mouth of food. "He caught word about my presentations today."

"Really," Tracy said. "Well I'm sure that that went smooth. Especially considering the ones today that everyone didn't expect to present the way they did."

I told Tracy earlier about this morning's essays and presentations. I mentioned about Donnie, the board, and how they all were going to make their final decision on Monday.

"Are you nervous?" Tracy asked.

"Nervous about what?"

"You know, your job as a teacher. The chance that they may or may not keep you."

I finished my sandwich and then crunched on the remaining chips on my plate.

"Tell me," I said. "Do you feel like they may, or do you feel that they may not keep me as a teacher?"

Tracy took a sip of her drink and wiped her mouth with her napkin. "Honestly, I think that you made a bold move with this whole assignment. Honestly, I think you had a lot of heart taking this to the measures that you took it. And honestly, I think you are gonna get just what you intended to prove out with this assignment."

"And you think," I said, holding up my hands in a posture that waited for her opinion.

Tracy stood up and came around the table where I was sitting. She sat on the edge of the right-hand side of the table next to me

"I think that if those students gave the kind of response that you said they did then that board ain't got no choice but to keep you and let you go on teaching."

I grinned, nodding as I looked at my plate in front of me.

Tracy cupped my chin, lifting my head up to look at her.

"Devon, I never said that I doubted anything that you've said along this project. Yeah, some of it seemed a little far-fetched at times, but never once did I say that I doubted you."

I grinned again with the expression of agreement.

"You are a strong, bold man. I know that if you set your mind to do something you'll do it in full faith. That's the person I fell in love with in college. I could tell then that you were just as confident as you are now, and when you asked me to marry you I knew the competence of a person that I was set to spend my life with."

Like a phrase from a poetic piece, so were Tracy's words. There was no doubt in my mind now that this woman had my back.

I stood up. "Thank you," I said, hugging her. "Hmm, thank you… for all the times I…" I paused. I had done a lot on this journey of trying to get to where I am now.

I overrode Tracy's disposition on many accounts, but now things were aligning and coming into perspective. I knew Tracy had my back in all that I did, but to hear her validate that at this moment set the tone for the whole outcome.

I looked at Tracy as I placed a hand underneath

her chin. "I know I haven't been all the way focused in the areas that I'm supposed to be. I know I have placed priorities in the wrong places, and have neglected you on many accounts. But, one thing that I am clear on at this point right now is my promise to you."

Tracy tilted her head slightly.

"Monday morning," I said. "That could be the end of my career at Lawrence Higgins High. Granted, the choice to place my job on the line could've been the worst thing I've done. But, you can be certain of this, and I don't need an interpretation for it. You are my world, Tracy, and when all the smoke clears I'm gonna take you on a vacation to give you the attention that you so need."

Tracy grinned.

"Won't nothing else matter," I continued, "because, at that point you and you only have my undivided attention. I'm not saying all of this as some sort of hyped speech. I'm saying it to tell you that I'll hang the moon for you with everything that's in me. Not because I want to, but because you deserve it."

Tracy smiled as a slight hint of tears glazed her eyes.

"Hmm, so it's like that, huh?" Tracy said.

I gave her a nod. "Absolutely."

Tracy grunted, glancing at my chest then up into my eyes. "All right, I guess you have proven your point."

I bowed my head to that.

"I guess you all right when you wanna be," Tracy teased. "But, I tell you what… Monday we'll find out the verdict. After that, we set plans on going far, far away."

I held out the palm of my hand. "On everything you love?"

Tracy stared down at my hand, smirking as she took me by the hand. "On everything I love."

We shook hands and I grabbed Tracy and hugged her tight.

# 29

THE NEXT MORNING I went by Darby's for coffee. I hadn't been there in a while so I thought that it would be good to stop in and show my face.

When I walked through the door I noticed that it was a little quieter than usual. There were customers sitting here and there, but it wasn't as custom would have it. Then again, I hadn't been there in a while. I walked over to the bar.

"Devon, my man," Darby said. "Long time no see."

I sat on the stool in front of the counter. "Yeah, been busy lately, Darb. You know, long days no rest. Get me a cup of my regular."

Darby gurgled in laughter at that statement. He walked over and fixed me an espresso. "Well you know, sometimes it's like that."

I picked up my coffee and savored a sip. The cup of coffee this time was a little stronger than usual.

"Man, Darb, what did you do?" I said. "You spike the coffee or something?"

Darby laughed, holding his sides. "Naw, naw, naw, Devon, you just ain't been here in a while."

I shrugged at that. I really hadn't been. I spent the majority of my time navigating this project with my class.

"So tell me," Darby said. "How's school treatin' you?"

"It's been a run, Darb," I said. "I had a couple of the students to present their papers before the school board."

"Really?" Darby elated. "How did you pull that off?"

I didn't want to go into a discussion about how I bargained my job. Darby was one who could go on and on with the details, and I didn't have the time for that.

"I talked with the principal," I said. "And, we worked it out to make it happen." I took another sip of the motor oil.

Darby started shaking his head. "I tell you, well… what did they say?"

"I won't know the conclusion of it all until Monday. Pretty much now, all we can do is hope for the best."

Darby started wiping the granite countertop ardently. "Well, you keep ya head up. I think you doin' a good job."

The bell rang from my phone. It was a text message from Tracy.

"Hey, Darb, I gotta run," I said, standing up and taking a few dollars from my wallet. "But, uh…

we'll be in touch."

"I hear ya," Darby replied. "Hey, keep it goin', hear?"

I gave Darby a thumbs as I passed through the door and out to the car.

I pulled up in the driveway after leaving Darby's. Tracy had said that she wanted to talk to me about something. I stepped out of the car and walked inside the house.

There was the smell of breakfast in the air. I smelled homemade biscuits and the sound of bacon frying. Tracy was standing in the kitchen scrambling eggs in a skillet.

"Hey," I said, walking in the kitchen.

Tracy turned her head and looked behind her. "Hey, baby," she said, stirring in the skillet. "You didn't waste no time getting up this morning."

I stood behind her, wrapping my arms around her waist.

"You were sleep," I said. "And I didn't want to wake you. I ran down to Darby's for coffee and to rap to him for a bit."

Tracy turned around as she laid the fork on a napkin beside the skillet. "Well, you could have woke me and had conversation with me."

I twisted my lip, staring Tracy in the face. She laughed at that last statement she made.

"Could have woke you," I said. "Yeah right, you and I both know better."

Tracy sniggled. She knew that if she was sleep, unless it was an emergency, do not wake her up.

"I'm playing," Tracy said. "I got this letter in

the mail." Tracy walked over to the counter and picked up an envelope.

"A letter?" I said. "From who?"

Tracy opened the envelope and she pulled out a folded white sheet of paper. "Alyssa."

"Alyssa? A letter about what?"

Tracy scanned through the letter.

"She's talking about how she apologizes for any misunderstanding or distance she may have created when she parted ways on the project that we were working on."

I folded my arms, frowning at the reasoning of that.

"Apologize for any misunderstanding or distance?" I said.

Tracy laid the letter on the counter and walked back over to the skillet of eggs. "Basically, she's talking about any misunderstandings that she may have created. She just wanted us to have a clear understanding, and know that there was nothing done out of spite against me."

"Okay, wait a minute," I said. "First of all, she had to write you a letter? Honey, y'all work at the same school. Was a letter really that serious?"

"Dev, sometimes that's the way some people can communicate better," Tracy replied. "And I just took it as her way of us trying to make peace."

"But, Trace, that's just it. Why did she bail out on you like she did?"

Tracy turned the skillet off and leaned against the counter with her arms folded. "Maybe that whole stir behind her uncle getting hit. I guess it kinda startled her. Maybe she was hoping that I wouldn't take her personal."

"Tell me, how do you feel?" I said.

"About the letter? It's, it's fine with me. I mean, I don't have anything against her. As long as we get an understanding that's all that matters to me."

I guess the awkwardness of it all is what had me feeling uneasy. On top of that, it astounded me how fast the news of issues spread between Madison, Jackson, and Vicksburg. I decided to just drop it all, and if Tracy was all right then I guess I was too.

Tracy walked over to me, patting me on the chest with both hands. "Devon, let's just let it go. I'm fine, she's fine, let it drop and move on."

I looked off with a deep concentrative stare. I laughed to myself within at how I was exaggerating the whole scenario.

I looked at Tracy, grumbling to myself. "You're right," I sighed. "Some people do communicate and get their point across better through writing. Fair enough, let's let it go at that."

Tracy gave me a kiss. "You hungry?" she said.

I grinned at her. "I could eat."

# 30

THE DAY OF reckoning had finally arrived. The alarm clock awoke me as I laid there in a peaceful sleep with my hands propped behind my head. I had waked up once, laying there in anticipation of the big day. Somewhere in that anticipation I drifted off to sleep.

I pulled back the cover and sat up on my side of the bed. Tracy still laid there asleep. It was Monday morning and the day of decision for me had come. I stood up and walked over to the closet to take out my clothes for the day. No suit or anything glamorous. I decided to dress like I would on any other day.

If I believed that I would still be a teacher of Sociology by the end of the day I might as well looked the part. Sure, I dressed a little more advance last Friday, but that was because we were presenting to administrative figures.

I walked in the bathroom and started my morning. I had waited for this moment all weekend. From the students presentations I really believed the ball would hold well in our favor.

Tracy walked into the kitchen. "Hey, good lookin'," she teased.

I was sitting at the table eating breakfast. I had cereal, two pieces of toast, and a glass of orange juice.

"Hey, love," I said. "How you doing this morning?"

Tracy sat her briefcase on the counter and walked over to the coffee pot.

"Oh, I see you made coffee," Tracy said. "I'm wonderful. Why didn't you get any of this?"

"Ah, just wanted juice," I shrugged, taking a bite of my toast. "I knew you would be in here in a minute so I made it for you."

"Aww, you so sweet." Tracy poured a cup and took a seat in the chair beside me.

"So, you ready?" Tracy asked.

"About ready as I'm gonna get," I replied.

Tracy laid her hand over mine. "I know you'll do great today."

I nodded. There was no need for me to fear now. I had made it this far so there was no point in looking back.

"Hey," Tracy said, nudging my hand. "Look at me."

I looked up from my cereal bowl.

"I am so proud of you," Tracy said. "Your dedication, hard work, fighting through adversity, it's all going to pay off."

I smiled. "Thanks, sweetheart." I stood up and picked up the cereal bowl and saucer. "I know it'll all work out. I have faith that it will."

I put the dishes in the sink and walked over to the counter and grabbed my book bag.

"I'm out, babe," I said, kissing Tracy on the cheek. "You have a good day too, okay."

Tracy stood up and gave me a kiss and a hug. "Hmm, I will. I'll talk to you later. Hey… remember you got this."

I grinned and turned to walk out of the door.

Sitting in the car in the parking lot of Lawrence Higgins High School, I prepped myself for what lay through those entrance doors. I wasn't so much afraid as I was in high anticipation of the school board's ruling. The millions of questions that passed through my head.

I remember Dr. Spartz once said to me, *suspense is an enigmatic foresight to the soul that can either be depicted as an adrenaline for eagerness or a confident outcome of high and great expectations.* In a lot of ways he may have been right. But, time would tell. I grabbed my bag and headed toward the building.

"Hey, Devon," Judy said as I walked into the office.

"Have you seen Mr. Donnell?" I asked.

"I think he is in his office. Did you want me to give him a buzz?"

"No, that's okay. I'll walk over to his office."

I walked out the door and across the hall to Mr. Donnell's office. The moment of truth of when a man shows what he's really made of.

"Come in," Mr. Donnell said.

I walked in his office. There were no board

members. It was just Mr. Donnell sitting at his desk flipping through a packet.

"Hey, Mr. Donnell, did I catch you at a bad time?"

Mr. Donnell checked something off on the packet with his pen. "Ah, just going through these forms from this packet the superintendent sent to me. Come on in."

I came in and took a seat in the chair in front of his desk.

"So," I said. "Any word from the board?"

"Yeah," Mr. Donnell replied, glancing at his watch. "They told me that they would be here at a quarter till so, we still got five minutes or so."

There came a knock at the door.

"Come on in," Mr. Donnell said, squinting as he read through a page on the form.

The door opened and Donnie Reagan came walking in.

"Mr. Reagan," I elated. "Good morning to you, sir."

I shook his hand firmly. Mr. Donnell shuffled the pages of the packet, standing up swiftly.

"Mr. Reagan, it's good to see you," Mr. Donnell said. "We're glad that you could make it."

"Well, I'm glad to be here too," Mr. Reagan replied.

"Please, have a seat there," Mr. Donnell said, motioning him to the chair that I was sitting in.

They both took a seat and I grabbed a chair that sat over in the corner. Mr. Reagan opened his briefcase and pulled out a manila folder.

"So," Mr. Donnell said. "What did you come up

with, or is any of the other members coming?"

"Oh no," Mr. Reagan replied. "I told them that I would take care of it."

Mr. Donnell nodded. He then turned and looked at me.

"Devon, do you have someone to cover your class?" he said, alarmed.

I turned and looked up at the clock on the wall. "Uh… no sir," I said, rising to stand up. "I guess I need…"

"Okay," Mr. Donnell said, flagging me with his hand to stay seated. He turned and picked up the phone on his desk. "Hey, Judy, see if you can get someone to cover Mr. Waters Sociology class for him for a while. He's here in my office in a meeting."

Judy agreed and Mr. Donnell hung up and turned his attention back to Mr. Reagan.

"Sorry about that, Mr. Reagan," Mr. Donnell said. "You were saying?"

Mr. Reagan opened his folder and pulled out a sheet of paper. "Yes, well… the other members and I read through the essays and we found a lot of very, very interesting things."

Chills frizzled across my shoulders.

"First," Mr. Reagan said. "There was that question of what chapter study blazed this whole assignment? Then, came the question of how this whole assignment could be integrated in order to draw a meaningful correlation in the subject of Sociology?"

"Mr. Reagan," I said, raising my hand. "If I may, I can answer those questions for you."

Mr. Reagan motioned with his hand for me to proceed.

"My first period class was totally disturbed with that scenario of the student hitting the teacher. What's more, the student did his essay assignment over a celeb producer at a charity event. But, here's the kicker to it, that same student was pulled out into the hallway where his teacher said, or did something to him that caused him to react."

"Yes, Mr. Waters," Mr. Reagan said. "We know that, but what does that…"

"That brought on this question," I said, raising a hand. "The class was in an uproar behind the whole commotion of a student doing a report over a celebrity who did a notable deed at a charity event."

I turned my chair toward Mr. Reagan.

"So," I continued, "since we were doing a chapter on social identity, the concept of 'I Am' staged from that."

Mr. Reagan raised an eyebrow. The principal, Mr. Donnell sat there in his seat, posing as an innocent bystander.

"I asked the class to consider something," I said. "I asked them if you could be anyone in any field, then what would be your stance to accredit to the celebrity arena. I'm not talking about some place in box office or red carpeted screen. If you could see yourself as a life coach, parole officer, artist, or maybe a nurse, then you have just as much a right of prominence as anyone you see on the other side of the screen."

Mr. Reagan nodded his head. I believe that he was starting to see the picture.

"That, Mr. Reagan, is where the 'I Am' concept derived from for this assignment. My whole objective and intent was to move my class away from the focus of the celebrity record producer and toward them searching inside and seeing what makes them great. If you were to say I Am Nathan the artist or I Am Emily the life coach, then that gives perfect definition to their character thus, making them important people."

I reclined back in my chair, resting my words on that thought. Mr. Reagan sat dumbfounded in his seat, as did Mr. Donnell. In my mind at this point it made no difference whether I was winning or losing. I was certain in my logic, and I believed that this concept of 'I Am' allotted for everyone to be great and awesome people.

"Tell me, Mr. Waters, what makes you so sure that everyone should view, or sees the world as that?" Mr. Reagan said.

I leaned forward in my seat. "Because, Mr. Reagan, we all have a chance to shine as a star. You, me, Mr. Donnell, we all have that right."

"And I assume that through this assignment you are expecting us to believe this and accept this all as true?"

I shrugged, raising a hand. I could feel the pressure in the room. I was giving my all, and being blatantly honest as I knew how.

"I see," Mr. Reagan said. "Well, the verdict is in, and the board and I have drawn a decision on the whole matter."

I leaned my arm on the desk, slightly tapping my fist. This was either the best day or the last day of my life here.

"Are you sure you want to risk your job for this matter?" Mr. Reagan said. "I mean, is this paper, this assignment that dear to you that you would risk your career for it?"

"It's either gonna make me or break me," I replied.

Mr. Reagan smirked, holding up the sheet of paper in his hand as if to read it.

"Devon Waters, the board and I reviewed all of the students' papers, we all deliberated and gave much thought from a collective and critical thinking standpoint. From a collective vote and a collaborative decision made, the board and I rule…"

I stared, not batting an eye. Mr. Donnell leaned forward on his desk, holding his breath.

"That this was a well thought-out, very thought-provoking, critical thinking assignment, and you, Devon Waters… did a very fine job in exercising the class's minds to think."

I gave a sigh of relief, slouching back in my chair. Mr. Donnell leaned back in his chair, sighing as well.

Mr. Reagan stood up.

"Excellent job, Devon," he said, extending his hand to shake mine. "And some of the other members of the board thought that it would be good if you could find a way to incorporate this assignment throughout the school."

I stood up and so did Mr. Donnell.

"That sounds like a good idea," I said. "And I believe the star-in-you concept would be great in bringing out the best in all the students."

Mr. Reagan picked up his briefcase and placed the manila folder back inside. Locking it, he turned and walked toward the door.

"Gentlemen, you all have a good day."

I scurried to stop him.

"Uh, Mr. Reagan, I am a bit curious about something. What did Mr. Buckley say, and what happens to Jackie now?"

Mr. Reagan grinned.

"Well, Devon, I did have a talk with Mr. Buckley, and he explained to me what happened."

I shoved my hands in my pockets. I had been waiting on this moment for a long time.

"When Mr. Buckley pulled Jackie out of the classroom, it was to offer more critiquing to his paper. Or so he thought. He mentioned about how he had done an oral review after the presentation in class, and how he was getting further complications from Jackie."

I raised my eyebrows. That must have been the reason why Jackie remained silent the other day when I went and talked to him.

Mr. Reagan rested his briefcase on Mr. Donnell's desk.

"So after all the students had read their papers, he asked Jackie to step out in the hall to speak to him. When they were out in the hall, Mr. Buckley gave him some suggestions and ways he could make his paper better next time."

"So why would he hit him?" I asked. "There's nothing wrong with offering corrections."

"And that's true," Mr. Reagan replied. "To offer it in a more personal manner, saving the student the embarrassment was the reason he asked him to step out in the hall. However, where Mr. Buckley faltered at was in the overzealousness of his tips and suggestions."

"Which is," I said, motioning a response with my hand.

Mr. Reagan straightened his shoulders as he placed his hands in his pockets.

"He misinterpreted the student's paper, and made the comment of how he should write and focus on more things that add value to his life. Don't waste life away by researching the trivial stuff, said Mr. Buckley."

I shook my head.

"Wait a minute, he considered a student doing a report on someone doing a charity event as trivial?"

"And that's where the misinterpretation comes in," Mr. Reagan said. "I explained to Mr. Buckley how the student's report wasn't so much focused on just the celebrity, but it was the act of benevolence offered by the celebrity."

"And in that kid's eyes that's what he saw," I added. "To him, it was a star doing charity for a town here in Mississippi."

Mr. Reagan picked up his briefcase. "Devon, the matter here wasn't about a racial discrepancy, as some may have found it to be, but it was about a student doing a report over someone who, in his eyes, was a star. I've spoken with Mr. Buckley in a meeting, and the board and I handled that matter with him."

I shrugged, rubbing my chin. It was a personal meeting, and for truth's sake I hope that it was handled in an orderly manner.

"As for Jackie, his actions put him in school suspension for an allotted time. However, we're going to shorten his time. He will have to pay for his actions, but we'll show some grace towards his suspension time."

I shook my head. It was good to know that they

were being considerate of him. I wasn't for taking sides; I just wanted fairness for everyone in this matter.

"Okay, Mr. Waters, and Mr. Donnell," Mr. Reagan ended, opening the door. "You gentlemen have a good day. And, let's keep this conversation here with us, okay?"

We both shook our heads. Mr. Donnell walked Mr. Reagan out, and I stood there in the hall watching them walk off. In my eyes, at the end of the day, it was about what was right for everyone.

I walked on to my classroom, with what little time was left of it.

The class sat in anticipation as I sat there behind my desk. The teacher that was covering for me left and we had ten minutes or so of class time left.

"So what did they say, Mr. Waters?" Nathan said.

I grinned as I bowed and shook my head. The class was on pins and needles for the summary of the matter. I pushed my chair back and stood up.

"Well, we talked and tried to draw a conclusion to all of this," I said. "The board reviewed everyone's paper, and they made a judgmental decision on it."

"Which is?" Anthony pleaded with his hand.

"They thought… hmm, they thought that…" I could have given a direct response, but I figured I would hold it just to build on the class's eagerness to know.

I held a fist to my mouth. "They thought, they thought that it was a good idea, and that you all did a phenomenal job."

The class wailed a cheer. Emily raced up to the

front, rushing my with a hug as she celebrated the achievement made.

"What about you?" Meagan said. "Are they gonna keep you?"

"Yeah," I replied. "I guess we'll continue with Sociology."

Everyone yelped another cheer. It felt so good to be able to add value to the lives of these students.

"All right," I said, waving my hands to calm the class. "I want to leave all of you with this one thought in these last few minutes of class."

The students sat up straight as they focused their attention on me.

"We went through a lot with this assignment," I said. "It took a while for some of you to catch on to the swing of it. But, you did, and it's because of you giving your best that you have now proven yourselves before others who are in authority positions that you are stars in your own right."

The class smiled, solacing the vibe of a job well done.

"The board talked to me about trying to get the I Am concept incorporated throughout the school, and you should all be proud because you had a part in it."

The class marveled. Everyone recognized, as I had themed during the course of this assignment, that we were now making a mark here in the school. When these students graduate that mark would carry on into their world.

"You should all be proud of yourselves," I said. "Because, I am so, so proud of you all."

The bell rang and everyone gathered their books to leave on that note.

# 31

AFTER SCHOOL LET out I went to see Jackie at the juvenile center. Hopefully this time we could make any amends and maybe come to some point of agreement.

When I walked into the building I was greeted by the same facilitator the last time I had visited. He greeted me with a disgruntle face, and a hope that I wouldn't come here to create a scene like the last time.

"Can I help you?" the man said.

I looked at his name badge. "Yes, Daniel, I would like to speak to Jackie Rollins if you don't mind."

Daniel was a middle-aged black man whose persona made him look like some hot shot police officer who was known for always catching crooks and criminals.

"May I ask what for?" Daniel inquired.

"He is a student from my school," I replied. "And, I was just here to update him on the status of the classes and curriculum."

Daniel grunted. I thought I did good giving him

a well articulated answer to his question.

"He gets his work and assignments from the school," Daniel said. "What else does he need to be updated on?"

"Well, it's in relations to a paper that he did," I said, scratching my head. "One of my classes and I took the time to do an assignment that was in relation to that."

I hoped that he didn't keep furthering with all of the questions. I didn't want to trap myself in some type of suspicion.

"I guess you can," Daniel said, turning around and walking to a door that led to another hall and doors. "Wait right here."

I stood there holding my folder, looking at the walls around me. To the right of me was a receptionist area, and the woman behind the glass was frivolously writing something in a tablet.

The door that Daniel walked out of opened and Jackie along with him came walking out. Jackie looked a shade better than the last time I saw him.

"All right," Daniel said. "I'ma give you fifteen minutes. Any ruckus and that's it."

I assured him that I wasn't here for drama, placing a hand on my chest. Jackie and I walked over to the lobby area and sat in two wooden chairs.

"So," I said, clasping both hands together. "How you doing?"

Jackie grumbled. "It ain't no paradise, but… I'm fine."

I nodded. "Well, Jackie, I know last time I was here we kinda got off on the wrong foot. I mean, I was just here to try to come to an understanding, and here for the facts that's all. I wasn't trying to shake or ruffle you or nothing."

Jackie shrugged as he bobbed his head. "It is what it is. Ain't no big deal."

I turned my chair toward him. "Hey listen, you know one of my classes did a project based on this whole situation with you and Mr. Buckley?"

Jackie curled his lips to the left. "A project? What, y'all ran outta stuff to talk about?"

"No," I laughed. "It's nothing like that. You see… my first period class was all shook up about what had happened. Everyone ranted and raved about their opinion on the matter, so I gave them an assignment."

"Assignment?" Jackie exclaimed.

"Yeah, I found out that you did your paper on a celebrity at a charity event in Canton. I gave the class a proposition and told them to do an essay?"

Jackie gave a puzzled look.

"I told them to consider themselves once they graduate and have moved on with their lives and have moved into whatever they choose to do, how could that area of their choosing give them the same recognition as a celebrity."

Jackie started laughing, leaning back in his seat. "Are you serious? Really, Mr. Waters, tell me that you jokin'?"

"I am serious," I assured. "The same type of hype, the same kind of attention stars get, I believe that whatever it is that they're going for they too can get it. Tell me, Jackie, why did you pick this record producer for your essay? He must have done something to get your attention?"

"I mean, he just a record producer," Jackie

shrugged. "A celebrity guy in the area, why not?"

"I know, but think about it. Beyond this, all of that with him being a celebrity producer and beyond the charity event, something about the idea of this guy being a celebrity caught your attention."

Jackie leaned forward in his seat. "Look, is there a point to all of this, Mr. Waters?"

"When you leave Lawrence Higgins High," I said. "What are your plans for the future?"

"I don't know," Jackie hunched his shoulders. "Prolly go to the air force or somethin'."

I stood up. "Is that what you really want to do, Jackie? Go to the air force? Because, I'm willing to bet you really want to do something else."

Daniel moved closer to our area slightly. I had been trying to maintain low tones to avoid disturbing the peace.

"Mr. Waters," Jackie said, standing up as well. "That's the only thing hittin' for me. Yeah, I could run and find some little job somewhere, but I ain't tryin' to spend the rest of my life wastin' it away on that."

I held up my folder. "You see this? This is a folder full of essay papers from a class of students who told me areas that they could build stardom in. I got a nurse, an artist, life coach, and even a parole officer in here. And, you know something else? They were all writing to present these papers before the school board in your defense."

Jackie raised his chin. I knew that through the front that he posed he was startled, and deep inside he knew a desire that he had that could contribute to his success. He was simply a kid who wanted to do something that would contribute to his life.

"Now," I said, shaking the folder. "You mean to tell me that I got a room full of students here in my hand and you can't think of nothing to attribute to your road to success?"

Jackie sighed. I knew that I was hitting closer to home with the whole matter.

"If I could do anything to contribute to my success," Jackie said. "Hmm, well… that sound real good, Mr. Waters, real good. But, you take a person like me, we don't have too many roads to stardom."

Jackie turned to walk off but stopped.

"I wasn't born with some silver spoon in my mouth," he said, turning back around. "Detention centers and juvenile facilities, that has been my life, and you know what else… that is my life."

"I don't believe that," I exclaimed. "Jackie, as much as you want me to believe that, I don't."

Jackie turned slightly, brushing off what I was saying.

"You wanna know what I believe?" I said. "I believe that you don't even give yourself a chance to succeed. You just accept stuff the way it is and you deal with it your own way."

"Man, that ain't even how it…"

"Yes it is, Jackie," I interrupted. "Look me in my eyes and you give me one good reason why you can't be a star on this stage of life. Forget about all of the yeah, detention is my life crap. Tell me, Jackie, tell me why you can't be a star in this life? I'm not talking about some rinky dink movie star, or nothing. I'm talking about you taking something that you love and succeeding at it because it's in that moment, Jackie, that you feel you're operating at your best."

Jackie looked at me with his head cocked to the side and his lips curled. In my heart I really believed that he just needed someone to take the time and ask him what made him excel in life.

"I don't have much time left," I said, looking in the direction where Daniel stood. "Tell me, Jackie, before I go, what is it that makes you feel like a star?"

Jackie looked down at the floor, pondering that question. If I could get him to answer me on that then I would be able to help him become the best he could be.

He held his head up, shoving his hands in his pockets as he looked me in the eyes.

"That's a good question, Mr. Waters," Jackie said. "And one day I may have an answer to it, but right now I don't."

I thought about how in many ways his response was synonymous to Anthony's when I asked him that question.

"Okay then, Jackie," I replied. "I'll hold you to that. But by the same token I'll be waiting to hear your answer to that question one day."

I walked on to the exit door with my folder in my hand. Exiting the door, Daniel took Jackie back to his room. There was a lot of grandness in that kid. If only he would open his eyes and let it shine forth.

Tracy sent me a text message telling me that she would be late getting home. She said that she had some paperwork that she needed to catch up on. I really was hoping that she would get home when I did so that I could share to her the good news.

As I road down the street to my house I noticed a herd of cars over at Jerry's house. I decided to drive on over and see what was going on. The vehicles were lined bumper to bumper on the shoulder in front of his house.

I parked at the tail end of the vehicles and stepped out of the car and walked toward Jerry's home. There were people gathered together in the front yard, and clustered together in front of the steps. It looked as if Jerry was holding one of his weekly meetings.

"So you see, that's why it's so imperative that we stay focused on the mission," Jerry said, talking to the audience that lay before him.

I stood on the outskirts of the crowd so that I wouldn't interrupt his speech.

Jerry looked out and over in my direction. "You take here, ladies and gentlemen," he said, extending his left arm in my direction. "One of our own teachers in the community. Devon, come and stand here with me please."

I froze. Standing there it felt as if someone had took a bucket of water and dashed it in my face. Yet, for the sake of this scenario, I walked on through the crowd of people and toward Jerry. I didn't have any idea what he was talking on, but I went along with it to see where we would end up.

I walked up the steps and stood by Jerry. Was I nervous? Somewhat. Something inside of me wanted to believe that this was an attempt at making a fool of me and my character.

Jerry laid a hand on my shoulder. "This is Devon Waters," he said. "And he's a teacher at Lawrence Higgins High School in Madison. Now, Devon, we're talking about deception, and how the deceptions of Hollywood to a large extent continue to corrupt our students' minds. Don't you agree, Devon?"

I agreed all right. Jerry wanted to make a joke of me. He drew his strengths to prevail when he had an audience of people to gleam fuel from.

"You're right, Jerry," I nodded. "It has had its role of deception."

"With that being said," Jerry said, holding out his arms before the people. "Devon constructed for his class a project that talked about stars and all that, and he gave his class an assignment that centered on that. Tell me, Devon, wouldn't you say that that kinda plays down the road to the deception in Hollywood?"

Jerry turned to me, waiting for an answer. I could see him trying to draw from the crowd in order to foil me.

"If you view it like that," I replied. "But in order to come to that conclusion, one must make sure that they understand the situation as a whole."

Jerry curled his lip. He was making a strong effort to demolish who I was before this crowd.

I put my hands in my pockets and looked out at the audience.

"Ladies and gentlemen, if I may, I would like to present my case before you, the people."

Jerry fixed his mouth to say something.

"A student at my school," I continued, holding up a hand to hush Jerry, "did an essay in his class, and had a conflict with his teacher. This misunderstanding caused the student to retaliate by hitting the teacher. He was reprimanded for his actions by being placed in a juvenile center.

"One of my classes was greatly disturbed by this situation and wanted to reach a point of clarity. It was said that the student did a report over some celebrity record producer doing a charity event in Canton. So, to draw my students' attention away from that whole incident, I gave them a proposition. I told them to turn their eyes away from that whole dilemma and turn them inside to tell me what makes them stars in this life."

The emotions and facial expressions from the crowd were mixed. There were nods, eyebrows raised, and some with nonchalant looks waiting for me to come to a conclusion.

"When I talk about stars and stardom," I said. "I'm talking about you taking something that you love and maximizing your potential thus, making you a star when you're operating at your optimum level of excellence."

Jerry frowned. "Wait a minute now, how is all that hype and talk on stardom going to exemplify your students greatness at the core level? Why not just push them to be great students without the hype of all that celebrity jargon?"

"Because stars, Mr. Kendell, are an image that they can identify with," I replied. "And to prove that out, my students' reports given on last Friday showed it. I had a class of students who thought that this I Am assignment was just a waste of time. Like you, it was jargon in their eyes. Until I watched a kid who lost her mother to breast cancer talk about how she was glad that I gave her that assignment, because it gave her that push to become a nurse in order to save other cancer patients."

The crowd of people marveled. I could tell by the surprised expressions covering their faces. My story about this assignment was slowly opening the crowd's eyes to the affect that it posed on my class.

"I had a student whose mind," I continued, "was totally locked up against this assignment. He talked the game of gab just like you, how this essay assignment was pointless. But little did I know that this same student aspires to become a parole officer. I don't know, Mr. Kendell, but in my sight and estimation that is an example of stardom."

A man out in the crowd raised his hand.

"How does the principal of the high school feel about all of this? Surely all of this has to be handled as it relates to what's best for the school."

"I'll tell you," I replied. "The principal, Mr. Donnell, wanted to call all of this off. He wanted to end it all, but I made him a proposal. I told him to get the school board down to the school that Friday morning and let the students read their papers before them. If after the reading he and the board felt that I had wasted time with this assignment, then he could replace me with another teacher that he saw fit to take my position and I would be out of a job."

The man looked at me, stunned. That was risky in his eyes for me to ask.

"Yes, me and my class reading their papers to show truth in this assignment verses me and my class reading and I fail and lose my job."

Jerry grinned, moving in closer to me. "Well, what did they say?"

I turned and looked at him, returning the grin. "We won, and the board wants to see how we can use that assignment to spread stardom to the students all throughout the school."

Jerry's enthusiasm dimmed. That was not the

answer that he was hoping for. In the quest to bring me down before the people, he watched the pendulum swing in the other direction.

A lady in the crowd raised her hand. "So, you risked your job at the expense of an assignment?"

I inhaled deeply. "Yes, ma'am, I did. Because in my heart and mind, we are all stars. The message and whole essence of the I Am assignment is to show that a star is simply someone who maximizes their potential. And this potential is shown best when a person is given a proper environment for it to flourish."

"Now, wait now," Jerry said, flagging his hand. "You keep talking all this about stars and you know that people's minds are going to automatically gravitate to that celebrity crap."

"No, Jerry," I exclaimed. "You gravitate that role to celebrity. You come out here time after time holding these meetings and twisting the concept of my message. You, Mr. Kendell, hope that it all will bring me down, but now you see that I have succeeded and my message is clear. And now you see that the joke's all on you."

Jerry was appalled at that statement.

"Yeah, you got a few months in school on social culture and now you act like you got all the answers, but the inferiority that you hold is shown best when you have a group of people supporting you."

I stepped down off the porch. I turned and faced Jerry. "Jerry, I'm gonna leave you with this. You tried to ruin me, hoped that my message was in regards to me being someone else, but after meeting over and over to try to twist what I'm saying, now you're gonna have to see this."

Jerry raised his chin. "See what?"

"See how your plan to bring me down failed," I replied. "See how all of these people here watched me make a bold move and succeed, and see how after all this time you are gonna have to take the fall for this all by yourself."

I turned around and started walking through the crowd.

"And once again you come barking up the wrong tree," Jerry said. "Then the heat is on and now you want to bail out."

I stopped. Turning back around, I walked back in Jerry's direction. When I was at the edge of the porch I turned out and faced the people.

"I could stand here all evening," I said. "And I could have a big dispute here with Jerry, but I'm not. I've made my point and message very clear. My intentions were never to mislead, or to give out the wrong perception. I've presented my case before the school board, and I've presented it here before you.

"If after giving my story on the whole matter prompts you to find fault, well, I can't really do anything about that. All I know is that I've watched this project bring out some wonderful things in a group of great students. Not only that, but it opened the eyes for the school board and let them see the grandness of it too."

I held out my arm, turning and facing Jerry. "Jerry here, in my opinion, is someone who poses as a teacher and community activist that rallies the town in a picket sign mentality when he feels that the community is in danger."

Jerry frowned, holding his head to the side and

giving a grimacing stare.

"That's fine and all," I continued, "but, before you resort to go there it's important to make sure that all of the elements of fact are in place. Otherwise, you can make yourself look like a scholastic genius who's climbing the ladder of intellectually persuasive speech only to find out when he gets to the top of that same ladder, it's against the wrong building."

Everyone clapped. I started back walking to my car not turning back but leaving Jerry to think about that. The crowd started scurrying and chattering with one another, carrying on as if the meeting was over with.

The truth of the matter is that it was. I may have not had been clear on many things, but Jerry and all of those people knew my objectives and intentions. That was something that Jerry could picket sign around too, along with all of his other philosophies.

# 32

THE FRONT DOOR opened and Tracy came walking through it carrying her briefcase, a school bag, and two notebooks under her arm. I rushed off of the couch and scurried to help her. I had fallen asleep on the couch after leaving Jerry's house.

"Hey, babe, let me help you with that," I said, grabbing the bags out of her hand.

I sat the bag and briefcase on the kitchen table, and Tracy stacked the notebooks on the counter. Tracy looked exhausted. I figured that the bulk of her school work had overtaken her day.

"Are you just wrapping up the day?" I said. "It's almost six-thirty."

"Yes," Tracy feigned. "I had some deadline paperwork that I had to get turned in today."

I placed a hand on her shoulders as we took a seat on the couch.

"Have you eaten anything yet?" Tracy asked.

"No, I've been sitting her kinda waiting on you. I had just fallen asleep before you came."

Tracy patted my knee. "How did your day go?"

I churned with excitement all over again on the inside. This moment here is what I had been waiting on since this morning.

"Well, it's like this," I said. "We met together this morning, Mr. Donnell, a member of the board, and I, and we talked over the verdict that the board had come up with."

"What'd they say?"

"The members reviewed the essay papers from the students, talked them over, examined the papers, and they made their decision."

Tracy held out her hand, implying for an answer.

I dropped my head, grinning slightly with my eyes closed. "They said… hmm… Tracy, they said…"

"What did they say, Devon?" Tracy chimed, shaking my knee.

"They said… that… the assignment was well done!" I exclaimed, raising my head with excitement on my face. "And, they want to try and spread that I Am concept in the school."

Tracy leaped over and landed in my lap. "Are you serious?"

"Yeah," I nodded. "I'm serious."

Tracy wrapped her arms around me and hugged me tight. "Honey, baby," she said, pecking my lips with kisses. "We did it. Babe, we won."

I gazed her in the eyes. "Yeah, we did, and I couldn't have pushed in all of this if I didn't have you here beside me along the way. Thank you, Trace for having my back all along the way. I love you, girl."

Tracy caressed my face. "And I thank you for

sticking your grounds and not giving up. And, I love you, boy."

I kissed my wife as I thought on all the work, effort, time, and belief that it took to get here. It was a battle, but it was definitely one worth fighting."

# 33

"AWW, THANK, Y'ALL," I said to the class the next morning.

My first period class pulled together and got me a thank you card and a plaque with a poem engrafted on it that talked about greatness.

"Thank, y'all. Hey, y'all are great too."

Meagan walked up to the front of the room and stood in front of me.

"Mr. Waters," Meagan said, tears filling her eyes. "Thank you for allowing me a chance to search on the inside of myself and tap into my greater self. You know, especially with the loss of my mom and all. I knew that I wanted to do something great with my life in honor of her, but this assignment allowed me the chance to let me know that I can do great things as a nurse because I am great."

Meagan rushed in my arms with a hug, sniffing as the tears rolled down her cheeks. As she stepped back I placed my hands on both of her shoulders.

"You're a good kid, Meg," I said. "And in this

life wherever you are when you graduate and move on from here, remember that you are a great person who is destined to do great things."

Meagan nodded her head. She turned around and returned to her desk.

"And that's what I want to say to all of you," I said. "This assignment wasn't just something that you do today and forget tomorrow. All of you are great, and as I've said before, stardom isn't just hidden in some kind of a Hollywood icon. You all are great people that are stars on this stage of life. Don't limit yourself, and what you do, because if you can take the time to learn the craft, learn the talent or skill, and if you can master it, you are a star."

The bell rang. The whole class stood up and walked to the door. Several of the students gave me a hug as they walked out.

"Mr. Waters," Anthony said, standing in front of me. "Thank you, man."

He gave me a thumbs up and shook my hand. As he walked out of the door, I thought to myself how this was definitely one of the best days of my life.

I stood out at the bus loop when school was out talking to several of the students. I also watched how the kids transacted with one another, and I also reflected on how there was something great on the inside of all of them.

Remembering back some time, I thought about that desire to be a hero that kindled deep within. It was during that time when I had a dream that sort of shook me up. I remember when I talked with Dr. Spartz about the dream that I had. He helped me to unfold it piece by piece, and told me that my dream could be a leading to something deeper than just the disturbance that it gave me. Maybe that assignment and what it is was meant to accomplish set the stage to bring out the hero that I longed for.

"Congratulations," someone said from behind me.

I turned around and there stood Dr. Spartz and Mr. Donnell.

"Dr. Spartz," I said, shaking his hand. "What are you doing here?"

Dr. Spartz smiled. "I had some things I needed to talk over with the counselors about the program for the Wise Students Wise Decisions."

"Okay, how's that going?"

"It's going quite well actually," Dr. Spartz said. "A lot of the students are catching on, and it looks like if they keep pressing forward with it on the path that we've set then they're on the right road to success."

I nodded. Mr. Donnell reached in his jacket in the inner pocket and pulled out an envelope.

"Here you go," Mr. Donnell said. "This is a letter from one of the students here for you."

I took the envelope. It was from Jackie.

"Uh, thank you," Mr. Donnell said. "I'm real proud of you, Devon. I know that that with the board was a risky move, but you dared to succeed in it."

I grinned. Daring was exactly what it was, especially with putting my job on the line.

"My hat's off to you," Mr. Donnell said. "Job well done." He turned and walked back inside the building.

Dr. Spartz grinned at us. "You know, Devon, I

think that hero that you and I talked on a little while back has finally shown himself in this matter."

"I do too," I laughed, recalling my previous thoughts. "I guess it just took a little time and the right circumstances to set it up."

Dr. Spartz chuckled. "Well, I think you're going down the right road. That message of stardom and the stars that can be brought out of every individual is what needs to be shared to everyone."

I agreed. Dr. Spartz shuffled his notebook and he held it in his other arm, holding it underneath it.

"Devon, I have to run," Dr. Spartz said. "I'll be back on next week some time."

We bided our farewells and I continued to stand there. I opened the envelope and unfolded the letter to read it.

Mr. Waters

I know you told me to get at you when I got my stuff together. You asked me what makes me feel like a star. When I first heard that I thought it was a bunch of b.s. People being stars doing ordinary stuff was one of the dumbest things that I ever heard. But as I had time to think about it some things started to make sense in my life. So I asked myself what makes me feel like a star or like you said if I could call myself a star in any area what would it be? For me I would have to say maybe a entrepreneur or something. I kind of want to do my own thing. So maybe a entrepreneur with my own personal training business. I kind of like fitness and all that. That's kind of weird for a hardhead like me. But maybe I will grow up one day and get my stuff together. So here it go. Maybe I'll see you when I get out of this shh...place. You thought I was going to go there, didn't you? Well, see you on the outside Mr. Waters. Tell the class thank you for the support. That's whats up. –Jackie

I grinned, looking at the letter and thinking of how underneath all of the adversity there was still a light. Even though Jackie considered himself a juvenile delinquent, he was really just a kid that needed direction in his life. Sure, there were some students whose case was a little more extreme than his, but if I could reach them I knew that I was doing my job. In my eyes, it was the hero I saw on the inside of me.

I folded the letter back up and stuffed it in the envelope. A majority of the students had cleared out so I went back inside to get my stuff and call it a day.

Walking back out and heading to my car, I stopped and thought about how this had been a pretty phenomenal past couple of days. My students were on the right track for the most part, and this spreading of the I Am concept we could definitely maximize more students one life at a time.

Jerry Kendell and his blurred concept of stars and stardom was just a misinterpretation of greatness that rested in each one of us. Not just in the students in this school, but in all of us as a society and world.

I started back walking on to my car.

"Where you going, cutie?" a voice said behind me.

I turned around and it was Tracy standing there with her arms folded.

"Tracy, where did you come from, and what are you doing here?" I said.

Tracy took a step forward and locked her arms around my waist. "Nothing, here to check up on my man."

I sniggled. "Check up on your man. Ooh, I see, well uh, how did you get out of work so soon? Usually I'm coming to hunt you down."

"Well, looks like the roles have switched haven't they?" Tracy replied, smiling.

I started back walking as Tracy wrapped her arm around mine and walked with me.

"I see you got gift bags in your hand," Tracy said. "What you got?"

"So now you wanna know," I grunted.

"Yes, I want to know. You be all up in my business when I get off work so yeah, I wanna know."

I started laughing. Tracy did have a point. I did corner her that day she came home with shopping bags.

"If you must know," I said. "My class gave me a card and a plaque."

"Look at you," Tracy replied. "I guess you all right."

I chuckled as we continued to walk. Tracy could be funny when she wanted to be.

"So, now you know you owe me?" Tracy said.

"Huh?" I replied.

"The assignment is done, all the battles and all are over, you owe me."

We stopped. I knew what she was talking about, but I hinted a peculiar face just to ruffle her up.

"Trace, what are you talking about?"

"I'm talking about my vacation," Tracy replied, slapping my shoulder.

Tracy started back walking. I wrapped my arms

around her, stopping her as I hugged her tightly.

"I'm playing, babe," I chuckled. "I'm playing, I'm playing. Now, what did you come up with?"

Tracy turned around and faced me. "I was thinking about going down to Cozumel. You know, soaking up the sun, relaxing and all that."

I bobbed my head. "Cozumel, okay, that sounds like a plan." We started back walking again.

"I was thinking," Tracy said as we walked. "You know, maybe it's time for us to have our own kids. I mean, we both deal with students every day, why not have children of our own?"

I stopped. I gave Tracy a puzzled look. "Hmm, that's a big step for us at this level in our career. Are you sure you're ready for that now?"

Tracy gazed in my eyes. "On everything you love?"

She returned the same phrase that I targeted her with once before. I glanced down at the ground and then back up at her, grinning.

"On everything I love," I replied.

I wrapped my arm around Tracy's neck as she put her arm around the small of my back. We walked and I thought about how I wasn't just walking with a wife, a soul mate, or my better half. I was walking out in the parking lot of Lawrence Higgins High School with my best friend in the entire world. I wouldn't trade this moment for nothing, and not only that, but I wouldn't trade this woman for nothing either.

# Others books by

# SRB Publications

- **Mirror of A Star**
- **The New Art of Oneness**
- **7 Keys To S.T.A.R.D.O.M.**

**...and D.R.E.A.M.**

for more on these books and more inspiration of stardom visit www.thestarinside.com

**SHELDON R. SMITH** is the author of several books, and is the founder of SRB Publications. His books include *The New Art of Oneness* and his first novel *Mirror of A Star*. He was also featured on Spotlite Radio with his inspirational book *7 Keys To S.T.A.R.D.O.M.* He lives in Texas, and continues to inspire greatness in the lives of others. Sheldon loves to hear from his readers via email: sheldon@thestarinside.com

Author photo: SRB Publications

Made in the USA
Columbia, SC
26 May 2024